Ginger raced toward him, her deep green eyes wide with worry.

"Ty! Are you all right?"

Words stuck in his throat. How did he answer that? "Yeah. I'm fine."

Suddenly she was hugging him. He put his hands to her back, holding on. Somewhere deep inside he felt a seismic shift, a tilting of his once solid and level foundation.

"I was so worried."

"Nothing to worry about. Everyone was out of the fire before I got there, but the cabin is probably a total loss." He expected her to release him, but she clung to him tightly.

"I was afraid you wouldn't come back."

"You can't get rid of me that easily."

She pulled back then, her eyes locking with his. "But you're my only friend. I don't know what I'd do without you."

His heart raced erratically for a moment. "Are we friends?" He realized with a jolt that he wanted her as a friend, and more than that, as well. The thought scared him.

Books by Lorraine Beatty

Love Inspired

Rekindled Romance
Restoring His Heart
**Protecting the Widow's Heart*

*Home to Dover

LORRAINE BEATTY

was born and raised in Columbus, Ohio, but has been blessed to be able to live in Germany, Connecticut and Baton Rouge. She now calls Mississippi home. She and her husband, Joe, have two sons and six grandchildren. Lorraine started writing in junior high and has written for trade books, newspapers and company newsletters. She is a member of RWA and ACFW and is a charter member and past president of Magnolia State Romance Writers. In her spare time she likes to work in her garden, travel and spend time with her family.

Protecting the Widow's Heart

Lorraine Beatty

Recycling programs for this product may not exist in your area.

ISBN-13: 978-0-373-87876-5

PROTECTING THE WIDOW'S HEART

This edition published by arrangement with Love Inspired Books.

www.Harlequin.com

Printed in U.S.A.

Humble yourselves, therefore, under the mighty hand of God so that at the proper time he may exalt you, casting all your anxieties on him, because he cares for you.

—*1 Peter* 5:6–7

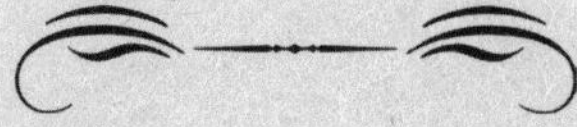

My Lord and Savior, who taught me a better way to use the gifts he gave me.

Chapter One

Ginger Sloan kept one hand on her son's shoulder and one on her small suitcase as they topped the wooden stairs hugging the side of the raised lakeside cabin and followed their benefactor, Mr. Nelson Cooper, across the wide deck. A patio table and chairs, two large rocking chairs and a big grill barely made a dent in the expansive space. All had been covered in heavy plastic to protect them from the weather. A quick glance past the railing revealed a large body of water sparkling in the moonlight. Its beauty escaped her. All she could think of was how isolated the place was, and what a fool she'd been to lose track of time.

Her seven-year-old son, Elliot, had begged for a break from the cross-country drive they were making from Shelton, Connecticut, to the small town of Spring Valley near Phoenix, Arizona. He'd been so good about being cooped up in the car for two days she'd wanted to reward him. So when they'd seen a sign for a Mississippi state park touting their expansive playground and a lake, she'd agreed to the small detour. But they'd lost track of time, and had made a wrong turn leaving the park, ending up on the far side of the lake after dark. Thankfully, she'd spotted some cabins and stopped to ask directions. But when she'd turned the key in the ignition, her car had refused to start, leaving them stranded and dependent upon the kindness of strangers for help and causing every nerve in her body to tighten in anxiety.

"I think you'll find the place real cozy." Cooper pushed open the door, smiling over his shoulder. "Let me get the lights for you."

Mr. Cooper, the owner of the cabin next door where she'd sought help, had been more than kind. He and his wife, Mae, had drawn her a map to I-55 and then, after her car wouldn't start, had offered to let her stay in the empty cabin next to them. While she was grateful, her fears far outweighed her gratitude.

"Mom, is that the same lake we saw before?" Elliot pointed to the water beyond the trees.

"Yes." She steered him into the cabin, her eyes taking a moment to adjust to the light. The main room was open concept with an L-shaped kitchen along the back wall. A long island with bar stools separated it from the living area. A massive stone fireplace with raised hearth, perfect for cozying up to, dominated the far wall. Windows, rising to the rafters, afforded an unobstructed view of the lake from the front. At the moment, it only revealed darkness, but Ginger allowed a quick second of anticipation to override her fear. The view in the morning would be amazing.

Mr. Cooper had stepped from the room briefly, muttering something about a water valve. He returned with a broad smile on his dark face and rubbing his hands together in a gesture of accomplishment. "Well, I think you're all set. The lights are working, the water is turned on, though I'd let it run a few minutes to clear out the pipes, and the pilot light is lit, so you should have heat soon."

Ginger pulled Elliot against her chest, keeping her hands on his slender shoulders. Mr. Cooper seemed kind enough, but it paid to be cautious. "Thank you, but are you sure this will be all right with the owner? He might not appreciate strangers staying here without his permission."

The man shook his head and smiled more broadly. "Don't you worry none about that. I know Mr. Durrant, and he'd be the first one to offer you aid. Besides, he's never here much. I take care of the place for him. Mae and I live out here full-time now that I'm retired." He rested his hands on his hips and glanced around the large room. "Let's see. I doubt if there's any food in the place." He walked to the fridge and pulled it open, then checked the cabinets, as well. "I'm going to go back to the house and gather up some things for you and your boy to eat. You get settled in, and I'll be back in a jiffy."

"Oh, you don't have to do that. We'll be fine. I appreciate all you've done, Mr. Cooper."

He smiled and pointed a finger at her. "Now, no more of that Mr. Cooper stuff. You call me Nels. We're friends now."

His words eased some of her tension, but she kept her guard up. Over the years she'd been conditioned to expect the worst at any moment.

"Until we know what's wrong with your vehicle, you need a safe place to stay and some food. But right now, you get yourselves settled in. We'll get your car towed to Zeke's in the morning, and let him take a look at it."

Towed? "How much will that cost?" The seriousness

of her situation slammed into her again. Money was tight. Really tight, and car repairs weren't in the budget. Neither was lodging or unexpected delays.

"Don't worry about that, either. Right now you and the boy get some rest. We'll tackle the big problems when the sun rises. Things always look better under the Lord's sunshine."

After Mr. Cooper, Nels, left, Ginger made a quick tour of the rest of the cabin. A master bedroom with attached bath was on one side of the cabin, a smaller bedroom was across the narrow hall with a full bath and laundry area next to it. She noted with interest that the small storage space beside the washer was stuffed full of sports equipment, which might come in handy to entertain Elliot tomorrow.

There didn't appear to be any other access to the cabin besides the front door. At least there was only one way in and one way out of this place. That gave her a measure of comfort. No one could sneak up on them unexpectedly out here in the wilderness.

"Mom, can I sleep in this room?" Elliot sat on the double bed in the smaller room, a big smile on his face. "It has fish in it." He pointed to the outdated wallpaper border along the ceiling depicting various kinds of fish flailing about on hooks. The bedspread was an ugly brown quilt with plaid fish in the center of large squares, and a brown-and-white checked border. Every item in the room reinforced the fishing theme. Only a man could appreciate such a decor.

"I think you'd better sleep with me tonight since we're in a strange place."

"Please? This room is way cool. There's even a fish lamp."

Ginger tugged on her hair. It was late. They were tired, and she didn't feel like arguing. She had too much to sort out. "Fine. But leave the door open so I can hear you in case you change your mind." Finding fresh sheets in the closet, she busied herself with putting them on the beds.

"Mrs. Sloan?"

The shout from the front of the cabin pulled a gasp from her throat and sent her heart thudding wildly. Nels. She'd forgotten he was going to return with the food. "Coming." She hurried out to the living area to find the older man and his wife busily unloading a box filled with a week's worth of food.

"Oh, you didn't need to bring so much. Milk and cereal for Elliot would have been fine."

Mae Cooper smiled and shook her head. "Nonsense. You might be here for a few days. I want to make sure you have enough food for that growing boy of yours."

Days? She hadn't thought that far ahead. What if the car couldn't be fixed? How would she get to Arizona then? Her head spun with the implications. Why did each new day of her life bring more unexpected problems? She'd spent the past two years living in fear of the next disaster.

"Now, then. That should hold you. We're going to get out of here and let you settle in, but if you need anything, anything at all, you come right next door and get me, all right?"

Mae smiled and patted her husband's shoulder. "Nels is a light sleeper, so he'll hear you if you call. I left our number on the counter for you."

After a quick bowl of cereal, Elliot scrambled into bed, eager to spend the night with the fish. Ginger returned to the kitchen to clean up, her glance falling on a tall, narrow cabinet in the far corner of the living room. Her throat seized up, trapping air in her chest. A gun case—rifles lined up in a neat row behind a glass door. Memories unfurled, yanking her back to the parking lot of a fast-food restaurant—she and Elliot waiting in the car as her husband, John, went inside. The strange popping sound. Realizing it was gunfire. The police. Sirens. Shielding Elliot from the horror. John being wheeled out on a stretcher. The hospital. Bullet to spine. Never walk again.

Ginger sucked in air, turning from the gun cabinet. Her life had changed forever that day. The surgeries, the complications that had dragged on, maxing out their insurance, forcing them to sell their home and destroying their credit. When John had died, she'd been left with over one hundred thousand dollars in medical bills and struggling to keep her head above water.

Slowly she turned, facing the cabinet again. She hated guns. Hated violence. A gun had destroyed her life and filled her with fear so deep and insidious she knew she'd never be free of it. Her only hope was to get to her mother's in Arizona. Maybe in the nice, safe town of Spring Valley she could rebuild her life and find peace.

Closing her eyes, she willed herself to calm down. She noticed a sturdy lock on the gun cabinet's door. She tugged on it, satisfied it was secure. She was safe. For the moment anyway.

Moving to the front door of the cabin, she locked it, checked all the windows and found them secured, as well. There was nothing else she could do. Back in the master bedroom she prepared for bed, trying to keep some perspective. The Coopers seemed like nice people. Kind and helpful. But she was stranded in the backwoods of Mississippi with strangers and without a car.

Reaching for her phone, she slid it open. She was almost out of minutes, but she had to call her mother and let her know where they were, and that they might be a few days late. "Mom?"

"Ginny, sweetheart, is everything okay?"

The sound of her mother's voice washed through her with a comforting warmth she'd long missed. Too many years had passed with no contact. Her fault entirely. Turning her back on the values and wisdom of her parents had seemed like freedom at the time, but only proved to be her downfall. But she intended to correct that now. "I've run into a little car trouble, and I'm spending the night at Shiloh Lake. It's near a small town called Dover, Mississippi. I wanted you to know in case."

"In case what?"

The concern in her mother's voice touched her heart. "Well…in case I have to stay awhile. I don't know what's wrong with my car yet. I'll find out tomorrow."

"Oh, dear. I hope you can still get here within the next week. I talked to my friend, and he'll hold off making a decision until he meets with you, but he really needs to fill the position as soon as possible."

"I know. I'll do my best."

"Ginny, you sound strange. Is anything else wrong?"

"No. Well, yes. There's a gun cabinet here in the cabin, and it brought back things I don't want to remember."

"Guns? Oh, sweetheart, are you safe there?"

"Yes, they're secured. But—" Tears sprang to her eyes and she swiped them away. "If only John hadn't put on that stupid uniform."

"I thought you said he liked being a security guard for that big office building."

"He did. But the police thought seeing John in his uniform is what set the gunman off. He thought John was the real police."

"Oh, Ginger. You never told me that. I'm so sorry. We have so much to catch up on. Hurry home to me. I love you, honey."

Her mother's words triggered more tears. "I will, Mom. Love you, too. I'm running low on minutes, so I'd better go. I just wanted to let you know."

"Sweetheart, I wish I could help you. I wish I had some money to send you but…"

"It's okay, Mom. We've met a nice couple who are helping us out. We'll be fine. Don't worry about us."

But worry was all she could do as she hung up, moved to the bathroom and prepared for bed. Rinsing the cleanser from her face, she stared at her reflection in the mirror. She looked pale as a ghost and tired. She couldn't remember looking any other way. Maybe, once she got to Spring Valley, she could spend a little time on herself. A stray lock of hair fell against her cheek. With an irritated grunt she grabbed a clip and fastened it in place. She'd tried everything to keep that cowlick at her temple under control. Cutting it off only made it stick out more. Curling and straightening never lasted more than an hour. As a result, it was forever hanging over her ear and brushing her cheek. Tugging it out of the way had developed into a habit. A professional stylist could probably help, but who could afford that?

Slipping between the covers, she turned her mind to getting some rest. The firm bed, with fresh sheets smelling like pine, wrapped her in comfort. The soothing combination beckoned her to let go of her fears and sleep. She could hear her son's steady breathing from across the hall. At least he would get some rest. She had too much on her mind. Such as how she was going to pay for car repairs, how she'd get to her mother's in time to take the much-needed job and how she was going to repay the owner of this cabin for using it. The Coopers had assured her there was no need, but Ginger knew firsthand the crushing burden of debt, and she refused to be indebted to anyone ever again.

Please, God. If You're listening this time, all I'm asking is to get to Mom's, so we can find a nice, safe place to start over.

The pain on his left side started at his thigh, traveled through his side and up to his neck. Tyler Durrant shifted his weight in the driver's seat and peered into the distance. The sign for Shiloh Lake was a few yards up ahead. He was almost at the cabin. He should have stopped and stretched his tired body hours ago, but he'd been too intent on getting to his sanctuary. He'd left Dallas on impulse late this afternoon and driven straight through with only a quick stop for gas and a package of cookies.

Slowing, he made the turn onto the narrow gravel road winding behind the twenty or so cabins lining the shores of the lake. What had once been a few remote fishing camps had grown into a small community of weekend cabins positioned close enough to keep residents from feeling isolated but far enough apart that you didn't feel your neighbor's eyes prying into your business. It was the perfect place for Ty to hide out and think things through.

A twinge of guilt pricked his conscience as he steered his car toward his cabin. He hadn't told his family he was coming back to Dover. He had a hard enough time with all his well-meaning fellow officers in Dallas. His family would be hovering and worrying, and he needed peace and quiet—time to figure out his future and make what could be the most important decision of his life. The cabin his uncle had left him was the perfect place. Quiet, private and peaceful. If he couldn't find his answers here, there were no answers to be found.

His medical leave was up at the end of the month. He had to decide if he would remain in law enforcement or look for work elsewhere. He knew what he wanted. He liked being a detective for the Dallas Police Department. But being shot had left him filled with doubts about his ability to do the job and stolen the sense of invincibility a police officer needed to function. He hadn't been able to pick up his service weapon since. What kind of cop could he be if he was too scared to use his gun?

Pressing his foot on the brake, he eased his SUV into the parking area beneath the cabin and stopped. Hands gripping the wheel, he sent up a quick prayer. *Lord, I need Your help sorting this out. I can't do it without You. Show me the future I should choose.*

His body protested as he pulled himself out of the car and retrieved his bag from the backseat. His thigh burned as he climbed the steps, the scar tissue pulling and stinging with each step. He inhaled a sharp breath. His wounds had healed completely, but overuse or lack of sleep brought back the aches and discomfort.

The fear and guilt, however, were always with him. He'd been over that night four months ago when he and his partner, Pete Steele, had made a follow-up call on a homicide case. The interview had taken an odd turn, so Pete had called for backup. But on the way to the car, a gunman had appeared around the side of the house, catching him by surprise. He'd hesitated, taking rounds to his thigh, his side and his neck. Pete had taken one to the chest and died. A death that Ty could have prevented if he'd acted more quickly.

On the broad deck, he paused a moment to select the cabin key from the assortment on his key ring, stealing a glance at the lake and the ribbon of light slashing across the water from the full moon. First thing in the morning he'd come out here with his coffee, or better yet, to the pier and soak up the quiet.

With one quick movement he unlocked the door and stepped through, and came face-to-face with a bat-wielding woman standing three feet in front of him.

"Stop right there. Don't take another step."

Ty stared a moment, then glanced around the cabin. It was his place. But he had no idea who this woman was. His surprise shifted abruptly to irritation. He dropped his duffel bag onto the floor. "Who *are* you and what are *you* doing in my cabin?"

"I have permission. And it's not your cabin."

Ty frowned and took a step toward the woman. She pulled back on the bat as if ready to swing it at his head. He held up his hands. "I'm not going to hurt you. I just want to know what you're doing here."

"I told you. I have permission from the owner."

"I'm the owner, and I didn't give anyone permission to stay here." His neck throbbed. He rubbed it with his fingers, trying to ease the stinging.

"Ha! That's not true. The owner lives out of state."

"Yeah. I live in Dallas." Ty took a closer look at the intruder. She was wrapped in a purple robe with baggy sleeves and tied at the waist. Her dark hair was trapped beneath the thick collar as if she'd tossed the robe on in haste. He guessed she was about five-eight, maybe thirty years old, but it was hard to tell when she had a bat poised over her head. For the first time, Ty was aware of the fear in the woman's eyes and the tense, protective curve of her shoulders. He took a step forward only to have her squeal and retreat against the wall, pulling a cell phone from her pocket.

"I'm calling the police." She punched in some numbers, all the while keeping a wary eye on him.

Ty lifted his hands in surrender and moved to the leather recliner, dropping down into it with a heavy sigh. His body was grateful for the softness. "Good. Chief Reynolds is a friend. He'll have this sorted out in a heartbeat, though I don't think he'll be too happy about you waking him up in the middle of the night."

The woman held the small phone to her ear, bat at the ready. "This is Mrs.... Uh, I need help at the cabin at the lake. The one next door to the Coopers. There's an intruder."

Ty held back the smile that found its way to his lips. That should bring the local law enforcement running. The ache in his side forced him up out of the chair. There was no place comfortable. He needed to stretch out on the bed. Fast. "Look, lady..."

A loud knock on the door interrupted him.

"Ty. Is that you?" Nelson Cooper peeked in the door, quickly coming inside when he saw what was happening. "Whoa. Mrs. Sloan, it's okay. Ty owns this cabin." Nels held up his hands, placing himself between them. "What are you doing here? I didn't expect you."

Ty watched the fear in the woman's eyes fade as she

lowered the bat, clutching the phone in her other hand. "I came home on a whim. Sorry. I didn't expect guests."

Nels shook Ty's hand, then moved to the woman, gently touching her arm. "This is Ginger Sloan. Her car broke down tonight, and she needed a place to stay. I didn't think you'd mind."

"Normally I wouldn't. But I'm afraid we'll have to make other arrangements." The woman's eyes, which he saw now were a dark green and covered with thick lashes, widened with worry. No. Desperation. Before he could speak, a small boy hurried toward them from the back, stopping at his mother's side, his eyes peeking over her protective arm.

"Mom?" His simple word held a boatload of questions.

"It's all right, Elliot. Don't worry."

"Do we have to leave? I like it here."

Ty glanced at his watch. It was nearly midnight, too late to make other arrangements. But he needed sleep. "Look, this is all a misunderstanding that we can sort out in the morning."

"We can sleep in the car." The woman raised her chin and met his gaze full-on.

He frowned. Did she think he was going to throw them out? "No need. You stay put. I'll bunk down at the boathouse. We'll talk tomorrow after we're all rested and calmer." He glanced at the boy, who he guessed to be a little older than his six-year-old nephew, Kenny. "Are you sleeping in the fish room?" A smiled moved the child's lips, bringing a light to his dark eyes. He nodded. "Good choice. That was always my favorite room. Watch out for Barney, though."

"Who's Barney?"

"Barney Brim. He's that fish on a stick sitting on

the dresser. He likes to wander around the cabin sometimes. I can't keep him in one place." The boy eyed him a moment, then smiled timidly. Picking up his duffel, Ty started for the door. Nelson spoke quietly to the woman.

"I'm so sorry for the confusion, Mrs. Sloan. Don't worry. Everything will be fine in the morning. You have my word."

Ty waited until Nels stepped outside before facing the woman again. "Don't worry about any further intrusions. I'll be down at the boathouse, and I promise I won't bother you. You're safe here."

For whatever reason, the woman's eyes lightened. "Thank you."

He started to leave, then turned back. "Uh, you wouldn't happen to have anything to eat in the house, would you?"

She nodded. "Nels and Mae brought enough food to feed an army. Take what you need."

Her expression had softened, but her defensive stance hadn't. She still held her son close to her side, as if protecting him from danger. Ty pulled a drink and a package of bologna from the fridge, then grabbed a bag of chips and the loaf of bread. "I'll bring this back in the morning."

At the door he stopped, taking one last look at the woman and her child. Those wide green eyes still held a wary shadow, but the boy wiggled his fingers and smiled.

By the time he said good-night to Nels and crossed the yard to the boathouse at the water's edge, he'd collected enough questions to keep him up all night. What was the woman's story? Why was she so frightened? And why had he wanted to pull her and the child into his arms and comfort them? Fatigue. It was the only explanation.

After a change into his sweats, he ate a quick bite, downed his meds and went to bed.

Lord, I need rest. I need peace. I can't have strangers in my life right now.

Closing his eyes, he drifted off, only to find a pair of pretty green eyes filled with worry and fear chasing him into sleep.

Chapter Two

The smell of fresh coffee permeated the cabin. Ginger had awakened rested and fortified to face the day ahead. It had been a long time since she'd had a good night's sleep, but last night she'd slept like a log, waking way later than her normal time. Maybe it was the profound quiet of the lakeside cabin, free from sirens and backfiring cars and all the unknown sounds that came with living in a low-rent apartment complex.

She poured a cup of coffee and spooned in a little cream and sugar. Elliot was still asleep, which gave her a rare and welcome quiet time to think and plan her next move. Moving to the expansive windows, she gazed out at the lake, now sparkling with sunlight. The old oak trees with their gnarled limbs, heavy with Spanish moss, painted a picture of serenity that beckoned her weary soul.

Grabbing a throw from the sofa, she headed out to the deck, removed the plastic covers from the wooden rockers and curled up, draping the throw across her lap. The air was chilly, but the knitted cover provided plenty of warmth. January in Mississippi was something she could get used to.

Another sip of coffee relaxed her enough to let go of her worries for a moment and take in the view. Below the deck the lawn sloped down to the water's edge. A long, sturdy pier stretched out into the lake. Trees hid the Coopers' cabin from view on one side. It was easy to imagine she was all alone on the lake. As her gaze traveled to the opposite side of the property, she saw the covered boat slip and the small shed attached. Was that the boathouse the owner had mentioned? It was tiny, too small to house a bed, she was sure.

The man—Durrant—was a good six feet tall. He must have been cramped in the little shed. He'd be eager to sleep in his own bed tonight, and she couldn't blame him. She and Elliot would have to find another place to go. Someplace cheap. But that still left the question of car repairs. She hoped it would be something simple like a battery or fan belt. Anything more she couldn't afford. Her gaze drifted back to the view, allowing her worries to slip into the back of her mind once more. Her soul craved peace like a thirsty sponge. She needed to fill up while she had the opportunity.

Movement near the water's edge drew her attention. Mr. Durrant was seated in one of the Adirondack chairs tucked between the trees. He stood, rolling his shoulders backward a couple of times, then reaching down to rub the side of one leg. Picking up a thick book from the arm of the chair, he started up the yard toward the cabin. He moved with a fluid, athletic grace, his long stride propelling him forward, but with a slight limp that piqued her curiosity and her compassion.

She was struck once again by his height. Perhaps the

limp was due to sleeping in the small boathouse. The least she could do was offer him a fresh cup of coffee. He'd been generous about letting them remain in the cabin last night. He could easily have ordered them out. She stood and moved to the railing, hoping to draw his attention. He stopped and glanced up at her with an expectant expression.

She hadn't realized what an attractive man he was last night. Her first impression hadn't been good. He'd been a tall, angry man threatening her world. Today he looked friendly and approachable. "I have coffee made, if you'd like a cup."

A small smile moved his lips. "I'll be right up."

She was pulling a clean mug from the cupboard when he tapped on the door. She motioned him in.

"That smells great. I tried to make coffee in the boathouse, but the pot is useless. Looks like some rodent chewed through the cord." He placed the thick book he carried at the end of the island.

The dark jeans and brown sweater he'd worn last night had been replaced with gray sweatpants and matching hooded jacket over a faded maroon college T-shirt. He was taller than she remembered, too. The angry expression was now relaxed and friendly, prompting her regrets again. "I'm sorry you had to sleep in that tiny boathouse. I'm sure it was uncomfortable."

He looked at her over the rim of his cup. "No. It's actually bigger than you'd expect. You'll have to come and take a look. No one stays there anymore, so it's not as well equipped as the cabin. How did you sleep?"

"Better than I'd expected, considering."

"Considering?"

Ginger clutched her mug between her hands. "We're

uninvited guests. I'm sure you're eager to have your cabin to yourself. As soon as I can make other arrangements, we'll be gone. I just don't know how long that will take."

"Yeah, well, we need to talk about that. Why don't we go out on the deck and sort this out?"

Her heart contracted. He was going to ask them to go. He'd be nice about it, but the end result would be the same. Homeless, broke and alone. Out on the deck, Ginger found the temperature had risen, and she no longer needed the throw. She took a seat in the rocker. Durrant pulled up the other one, angling it so they could talk.

She stole a quick look at him. He was a handsome man with thick brown hair that spilled over his forehead in an unruly fashion. But it was his eyes that captivated her. The bluest, clearest eyes she'd ever seen. Like a summer sky. With long lashes above high cheekbones, the angular, masculine planes of his face were softened by full lips and a chin with a slight cleft.

Despite his attractiveness, he appeared a bit gaunt, as if his frame was used to carrying more weight. The deep creases on either side of his mouth looked as if they'd been carved from pain rather than laughter. Her curiosity grew.

"Nels said your car won't start. How did you end up here at the cabins? Few people wander this far from the park or campgrounds."

Ginger quickly explained the circumstances.

"Arizona. That's still a few days' drive from here."

"I know. I need to be there by the end of next week at the latest. My mother has a job lined up for me. I'm hoping the car will be fixed quickly."

"Zeke Owens runs the best garage in town. And he's honest. He won't steer you wrong."

"That's good to know, but that's not my main concern." No need to be coy. The situation was too dire. "Mr. Durrant, I need to be honest with you. I'm in no position to pay you back for the use of your cabin. In fact, I have no idea how I'll pay for the car repairs. I have only enough money to get me to my mother's. If it hadn't been for Nels offering your place for the night, Elliot and I would have slept in the car." She braved a look at her host.

"Call me Ty. Mr. Durrant is my dad."

The kindness and sympathy in his blue eyes sent a funny tingle along her skin. She took a sip of her coffee to collect herself. "Ginger. It's short for Virginia."

"There's no one you can call for help?"

She shook her head. "My mom is on a fixed income. She sent me all she could afford." She could see the next question forming in the man's mind and hastened to address it. "My husband died a year ago. It's only me and Elliot."

"Mom." Elliot came onto the deck, hurrying to his mother's side. "I'm hungry."

She squeezed his hand, grateful for the interruption. "Good morning, sleepyhead. Well, let's see what we can do about that."

Ty watched mother and child leave the deck, his protective instincts kicking into high gear. Alone and broke. There was no way he'd ask them to leave the cabin now. His heart sank. His prayer time this morning had strengthened him, but it was ebbing away quickly. He needed time to sort out his future. He had a big decision to make, and he couldn't do that with people in his cabin. But he couldn't toss them out, either.

Father, what are You doing? I need Your guidance and direction. I need answers.

The grinding of gears and the roar of a diesel engine invaded the quiet morning. Zeke's tow truck had arrived.

Ty walked to the stairs at the end of the deck in time to see the massive truck backing up toward the small car in front of Nels's place. He hadn't noticed the late model sedan last night. Nels was already talking to the driver, so Ty contented himself with watching. The noise must have alerted his guests because they appeared at his side. He couldn't help but notice the contrast between the shadowed concern in the mother's pretty eyes and the bright excitement in the boy's.

"Cool. I want to go see the truck." Elliot started forward, only to be yanked back by his mother's firm grasp.

"You'll do no such thing. Stay right here."

Ty ruffled the boy's hair, nodding at Ginger. "Go ahead. We'll sit here on the steps and watch." He lowered himself onto the top step, gesturing for the boy to join him.

"But I can't see from here."

"Are you kidding?" Ty nudged the boy's shoulder with his own and grinned. "This is the perfect spot. You can see everything, and you don't have to breathe in any of those stinky diesel fumes."

Ty watched the proceedings, unable to take his eyes off Ginger as she went down to talk to Nels and the truck driver. Her body language revealed her distress. Her arms were wrapped around her waist in a protective posture. Several times she reached up to toy with a loose curl that bobbed against her right cheek. Even across the distance he could see her chewing her lip and the deepening frown on her forehead as her car was loaded onto the flatbed to be hauled away.

As she came toward him, he looked into her eyes and saw fear. His throat tightened. He recognized that look. It was the same one he saw in his own eyes each morning. Fear of the future, fear of what the next moment might bring. A fear that held you captive and challenged your belief in yourself and your ability to function. Being shot had left him paralyzed with fear. What had caused Ginger's?

He cleared his throat so he could speak. "What did he say?"

"Not much. They'll call when they know what's wrong. Oh." Her frown deepened. "My phone is out of minutes. How will they contact me?"

"Don't worry. They know me. And I'll check with them."

"Mom, look. There are ducks out there."

With the tow truck gone, Elliot had returned to the deck, looking for new diversions. He leaned against the rail and pointed at the lake. Ty joined him. "Would you like to feed them?" The boy turned to look at his mother, his expression filled with hope. Ty smiled at Ginger. She could probably use some time to herself. "I keep feed near the boathouse. I won't take my eyes off him, and we'll stay on the pier. Promise." He saw the hesitation in her eyes and knew the moment she decided he was trustworthy enough for the task.

"All right."

Ginger finished cleaning up the kitchen, then went out onto the deck to check on her son. She'd taken advantage of Ty's offer to help Elliot feed the ducks to grab a shower and straighten up. Leaning against the deck railing, she smiled at the sight of her son tossing food into the water. His giggles lifted on the morning air, landing in the middle of her heart with a warm swell. Elliot was always so serious. Hearing his laughter was an answer to her prayers—something she was relearning how to do. After years of being angry at the Lord, it wasn't easy to ask for His guidance. She was making progress. One small prayer at a time.

Another laugh captured her attention. A deep, throaty laugh. Her gaze shifted to Ty Durrant, who was now hunkered down beside her son pointing to the water. Elliot leaned forward. Too far. Ginger started to shout for him to be careful, but before she could speak, Ty took hold of his shirt and eased him back. He glanced up, and his blue gaze collided with hers. He nodded, then tapped her son on his shoulder. Elliot waved and raced toward the cabin.

"Mom! I fed the ducks, and the fish ate some, too. And there're turtles everywhere."

Her son's joy brought tears to her eyes, and a ray of hope to her spirits. Maybe they could find a new beginning. One where joy and laughter ruled, not anger and fear.

Ty came up onto the deck, leaving Elliot in the yard.

"Stay away from the water."

"I will, Mom. I'm going to look for more turtles."

Ty joined her at the railing. He'd removed his hooded jacket and pushed up the sleeves of the well-worn maroon T-shirt, revealing strong forearms. A sturdy black watch strapped across his wrist highlighted his nicely sculpted hands. She tore her gaze back to her son. "He shouldn't be down there alone."

"He'll be okay. I told him not to go on the pier without a grown-up. Does he know how to swim?"

"No."

"Well, the water's not deep at the edge. A foot or so. Worst he would get is wet and muddy, but I'll see if I can find a small life vest for him if it'll make you feel better."

"It would. He's all I have left." She could sense Ty's probing gaze assessing her.

"He's a great kid. He reminds me of my nephew. Maybe I'll get them together soon. Give Elliot someone his age to play with."

"You have family here?"

Ty smiled and nodded. "I was raised here. My dad owns the local hardware store. My brother and his family live in Dover, and my sister has her own construction company. I'm the only one who lives out of town. And I haven't been home in a long while."

"I'm sure they're glad you're back now."

Ty rubbed the side of his neck. "They would be if they knew I was in town."

Ginger turned to face him. "You didn't tell them? Why?" He turned away, resting his forearms on the railing and staring out to the water. Obviously he didn't want to discuss the issue.

"I have things I need to sort out. I can do that best alone."

"But maybe your family could help." If only she'd had someone to talk to, to comfort her when she'd felt so abandoned and alone, her world filled with anxiety and hopelessness

Ty shook his head, a slight smile on his face. "My dad would heap advice on my head, my mom would bake a pile of cookies and my brother and sister would harass me beyond endurance. I don't need that right now."

A sudden thought erupted in her mind. "You're not estranged from your family, are you?" She laid her hand on his forearm, acutely aware of the warm strength beneath her fingers and the steady pulsing of the blood through his veins. She told herself to remove her hand, but for some reason she didn't want to. "Because if there is, you need to sort it out immediately." Memories of the years separated from her parents because of anger and stupid pride flooded her mind. "Don't let another day go by, Ty. Don't waste time on petty grievances and misplaced pride. I know what kind of sorrow that can bring."

Ty turned to face her, his blue eyes filled with a tenderness she hadn't expected and didn't understand. He took her hand in both of his, enfolding her in a sense of warmth and security.

"I'm not at odds with my family, Ginger. I love them. I depend on them."

"So why don't you want them to know you're in town?"

He released her, turning to stare at the lake again. "Because what I have to decide, I have to do alone. My family knows my situation, but they can't help me with this particular problem. There's only one person who can help me, and so far he hasn't been forthcoming."

"Who's that?"

He grinned, deepening the crevices in his cheek. "The good Lord."

His words cast a shadow over her mood. "Maybe He's too busy to listen."

A frown creased Ty's forehead, causing a strand of

hair to fall over it. "He listens to the prayers of all His children."

He sounded so confident. But she knew otherwise. "Elliot. Time to come in." Back inside the cabin, she headed to the kitchen. As she passed the island, she spotted the book she'd seen Ty reading earlier. It was a worn leather Bible. Why hadn't God listened to her prayers?

Ty entered the cabin with Elliot at his side. "I'm heading to town shortly. Would you and Elliot like to tag along? We can stock up on supplies and check in with Zeke to see if he has a diagnosis on your car yet."

She wanted to find out about her car, but the thought of leaving the safety of the cabin, putting herself into unknown situations, talking to strangers, triggered all her old fears. She knew it was cowardly, but she couldn't help it. "No. I have things to do here. Besides, I want to wait for the call."

She reached for her cell phone, only to remember it was out of minutes. She needed time alone to gather her strength for what was to come. She thought about what Ty had said, about him needing alone time. That was something they had in common. But she had to have a phone. There was only one other solution—swallow her pride and ask for help. She'd done that already when she'd contacted her mother after a nine-year silence. Apparently, she'd have to swallow a lot more until she could get to her mom's and start fresh. "Could I ask you for a favor?"

"Name it."

"Could you have my phone loaded with more minutes? If you'll bring me the receipt, I'll pay you back."

"Sure. Hey, I just remembered. I have an old plug-in phone around here someplace, and the cabin's wired for it." He moved to the cabinet under the television, then to a lower drawer in the kitchen, finally pulling out a land-line phone. He carried it to the end table and plugged it into the phone jack in the wall. "I can call you on this if I need to. I'll give the number to the garage, too."

"Thank you." He seemed to think of everything. "I appreciate that."

Ty pulled his vehicle into an empty parking space in front of the Dover city government complex, turned off the engine and hopped out. His gaze fell on the items piled to the roof in the back of his SUV. If his instincts were correct, this was the sum total of Ginger and Elliot's possessions. His stomach turned queasy. They truly were homeless.

When he'd stopped by Zeke's earlier to check on Ginger's car, he'd noticed all the boxes and bags stuffed in the trunk and the backseat. He doubted anyone would mess with their belongings while at the shop, but better safe than sorry. He'd transferred it all to his car, intending to store it in one of the cabinets below the cabin until she left. Which, according to Zeke, might be a while. The car was in bad shape. The preliminary once-over indicated a transmission problem, which always meant big bucks.

Ty had made Zeke promise to call him first with the final assessment. Hopefully, he could find a way to tell Ginger, or better yet, have an alternative plan in place. He wanted to know what had happened to land them in this situation, but even in the short time he'd known them, it was clear that Ginger Sloan wasn't one who accepted help easily.

Crossing the parking lot, he pulled open the glass door and stepped inside the sprawling building that housed the police department and other city offices. The modern facility was a new addition since he'd been home last.

His main reason for stopping by was to check in with the local police, let them know another officer was in town. Technically, since he was on medical leave, he had no authority here in Dover, but it was common courtesy to make his presence known. More importantly, he wanted to see his old mentor, Chief Brady Reynolds.

Inside the building, Ty glanced around, getting his bearings. The reception area was large and spacious with several rows of chairs for waiting, many of them occupied. The information desk consisted of a large window above a wide counter. A hallway to the right extended the length of the building. Signs placed perpendicular to the doors directed residents to various departments. The sign above the hall to the left designated the police department.

Ty started toward the information window as two uniformed Dover police officers strode into the reception room and toward the front door. A cold vise clamped around his heart. A knot the size of a football formed in his gut. He started to sweat, his hands balling into tight fists at his side.

His mind struggled to process what he was seeing. People moving about. Phones ringing in the background. The tension and activity of a city complex. All of it so familiar. While he'd never worked as a police officer here in Dover, all stations had the same feeling for him. Home. Where he belonged. Now being here filled him with doubt and fear and feelings of failure and guilt. He willed himself to get control. He hadn't anticipated this kind of reaction.

Forcing a few deep breaths, he fought back the fear

and moved forward to the man seated at the information desk. "I'd like to see Chief Reynolds, please."

The man eyed him closely. Did he look as freaked out as he felt?

"Name?"

"Ty..." If he gave his last name, his family would hear about it before he could blink. "Just tell him Ty is here. He'll know."

After a quickly placed call, the man leaned forward and gestured to the right. "Down that hall. First door on the left."

With each step down the tiled hallway, Ty's anxiety grew. It was always like this. One minute he was fine, the next he was caught in a tidal wave of emotion he couldn't control. Maybe, once he'd made his decision, these anxiety attacks would disappear.

Chief Brady Reynolds met him at his office door. "Well, this is a nice surprise. I saw your dad this morning, and he never said a word about you being home." Reynolds shook Ty's hand and gave him a firm pat on the shoulder before pulling him into the office and closing the door. He sat down behind his desk, gesturing for Ty to be seated.

Ty eased into the chair, grimacing at a sudden stitch in his side. "That's because the family doesn't know I'm here."

Brady drew his eyebrows together. "You don't say. Is there a reason for that?"

Exhaling a heavy sigh, Ty lifted one shoulder. "I need time to sort things out. I can't do that if they're hovering all the time."

"I understand. So, what brings you here?"

His mentor's easy manner and warm smile chased

away the last of Ty's anxiety attack. "I just wanted to check in, let you know I'm in town. In case you need the assistance of a big-city cop. Someone with real experience."

Reynolds smiled at the teasing dig. "What I need is an officer who loves the town." Brady grunted and leaned forward, resting his arms on his desk. "This little visit have anything to do with the shooting?"

One of the reasons Ty had come to see his old mentor was his directness. He never beat around the bush. "Yeah. It does."

"How's that going? You look good."

Ty crossed his legs. "Physically, I'm almost back to normal. I need to build up my strength, but in another month or so I'll be good as new."

"And the emotional part?"

The scar on his neck started to itch. "Lousy. The shrink suggested I go someplace quiet to think things through. That's why I came here." The chief studied him a long moment.

"Ty, when an officer gets shot, it's not just the trauma to the body that has to heal, but the trauma to the spirit, as well. The ordeal can force an officer to accept that he's mortal, that a gun and a badge doesn't make him invincible. He may wonder if he can still do his job."

"And if he can't?"

"There are plenty of other law enforcement jobs besides walking a beat or investigating crimes. More money in the private sector, too." He leaned back, making the leather chair creak softly. "I had a tough time after my shooting. It was a simple flesh wound, but I doubted my abilities, and my sanity, at one point. I seriously considered putting the badge down forever."

That option was the last one Ty wanted to consider. “How did you get past it?”

“Prayer and determination.” He smiled. “Ty, I’ve known you since you were a teen, and I know you’ve wanted to be a cop your entire life. If ever the Lord created a man to be a police officer, it’s you. Give yourself time. The Lord will give you the answer, but in His time, and when He’s ready and everything is in place.”

Ty mulled over his friend’s words a short while later as he picked up a new prepaid phone for Ginger, then headed for his parents’ home. While he appreciated Brady’s confidence in him, it didn’t change the fact that Ty was in the grip of fear and guilt he didn’t know how to conquer.

Pulling into the driveway, he sat behind the wheel a moment, reluctant to face his mom. He’d chosen to come here while his dad was at the store. He could only deal with one parent at a time. Angie Durrant was standing in front of the sink when he entered. She glanced up and froze. Her face paled a moment, then brightened with a wide smile and moist eyes.

“Ty. Oh, sweetheart, what a wonderful surprise.” She wrapped him in a tight hug. “How are you? Are you all right?”

Ty nodded and stepped back. “Fine, Mom. All healed up.”

“I wish you would have warned me you were coming. I could have had your room all ready for you. It won’t take but a minute to freshen it up.” She started to turn away, but he caught her arm.

“Mom, I’m not staying here. I’m staying at the cabin. I got in late last night.” The look of hurt and disappointment on her face wounded him. “I need time to think about what I’m going to do next, Mom. I have to decide if I'm going to stay on the force or look into another line of work."

She nodded. "I see. Well, you know if there's anything you need, your father and I are always here for you."

"I know, Mom, and that's one of the reasons I'm here." He took a seat at the kitchen island. "I have a problem I may need your help with. There's a woman and her son at my cabin." His mother's eyes widened, and he quickly explained.

"Oh, the poor thing. What can we do to help?"

"I don't know yet. But I was thinking of maybe buying them plane tickets so they could go to her mother's."

"We can certainly handle that." She reached across the table and patted his hand. "Let us know when you decide what you want to do for them."

"I will." He stood and prepared to leave. "I'd like to bring them to church tomorrow, then come back here for dinner, if that's okay."

"Of course. I'm anxious to meet them." She followed him to the door, laying a hand on his arm. "Son, I want to help you. It hurts me to see you this way."

"I know. But I have to figure this out on my own, Mom. Don't worry. The Lord and I are working on it. I know He has a plan. He just hasn't told me what it is yet."

Chapter Three

Ginger dug out the box of small metal cars from the satchel containing Elliot's toys. "Found them." Her shout brought her son dashing into the bedroom.

"Thanks. I'm going to take them to the dirt pile. It'll make good ramps. They'll shoot way up in the air." He demonstrated with his hands and made a *gershing* sound through his teeth.

"What dirt pile?"

"The one down by the other deck."

"Other deck?" Granted, they'd only been at this cabin less than twenty-four hours, but her son had discovered every nook and cranny. All she'd experienced was the cabin and the deck. Maybe after lunch, she'd explore the grounds. She'd been longing to walk out onto the pier and maybe even sit in one of the inviting Adirondack chairs under the trees. The weather was cool today, but nothing like what she'd left behind in Connecticut in early January.

"I think you'd better drive your cars on the deck for now. I'm going to fix lunch, then you can show me all the things you've discovered."

It took only a second in the kitchen to realize Ty had forgotten to bring back the only loaf of bread. A quick search of the rest of the food revealed little else for a meal. While there were various options, each required an ingredient that was missing. Ty had been wise to suggest a trip to the grocery store. Maybe she should have gone along. At least then she could have picked up things her son would eat. Which mainly consisted of cereal, hot dogs and canned spaghetti. And of course, peanut butter and jelly.

Another thought leaped into her mind, sending her reaching for the notepad on the counter. She had to start a list of the money she owed Ty Durrant. Lodging, food, laundry detergent—she'd tossed in their dirty clothes this morning. Phone. She guessed at the amounts. Once she had some receipts, she could make a more accurate tally.

But in the meantime, no bread. The boathouse. Maybe she could go and get it. Or was that invading his privacy? She walked out to the deck. "Elliot, how does soup sound for lunch?"

"Yuck."

No surprise there. "Ty forgot to return the loaf of bread. Do you know if he locks the boathouse?" He shrugged, not taking his eyes from the caravan of tiny cars he was creating on the planked deck.

"Okay. Well, I'm going to go see. You want to come?"

"Nope."

Great. If she was going to break into Ty's place, she'd be all alone. Her heart pounded as she crossed the yard. What if he came home and found her there? Not good. It was only a loaf of bread. No big deal. Then again, look what stealing a loaf of bread had done to Jean Valjean.

The closer she came to the boathouse, the larger it appeared. She stepped onto the narrow wooden walkway connecting the covered boat slip with the house. Two large windows on either side of the door were coated with grime. The place was old and rickety, but a good size. Standing here now, she decided that maybe Ty wasn't as cramped as she'd assumed.

Swallowing her doubts, she reached out and turned the knob, startled when the door swung open of its own accord. She peeked in, surprised to find the place nothing as she expected. The boathouse was one large room. A twin bed tucked in an alcove against the back wall was unmade. Beside it an open door revealed a small bathroom. A tiny kitchen, consisting of little more than a sink and a counter with a small fridge tucked beneath, took up one wall. The opposite wall held shelves behind a rickety vinyl recliner that was probably one of the first ones ever invented. A small table with an out-of-date television completed the decor.

She exhaled. Well, she could quit worrying about Ty's comfort. The place might be small, musty and very old, but he had everything he needed. Her gaze traveled to the duffel bag partially open on the floor. T-shirts and white socks poked out the top. The dark jeans he'd worn last night were in a heap beside it. The sweats he'd worn this morning were tossed across the foot of the bed.

The intimacy of his personal things sent heated embarrassment into her cheeks. She'd come for the bread, not to snoop. Spinning around, she scanned the small kitchen, finding the loaf of bread on the counter near the coffeepot. Grabbing it up, she hurried out, shutting the door firmly behind her.

After lunch, Elliot gave her a tour of the grounds around the cabin, from the large lower deck with a hot tub to the pier and the boat slip and the picnic table nestled beneath a large oak tree draped with moss. The pleasant weather was the perfect invitation to take a walk along the pathway that followed the banks of the lake.

When they returned to the cabin, Elliot opted to stay in the yard and look for turtles while Ginger went inside to wait for the call from the garage. She'd planned on staying close to the phone, but her time with her son was too important to miss. The phone rang as she walked into the living room. Her stomach tightened as she lifted the receiver.

"This is Jeb from Owens Automotive Repair."

She struggled to find her voice. "What's the verdict about my car?" As she listened to the man's report, her knees buckled, sending her sinking onto the sofa. "Thank you. I'll let you know what I decide to do."

She hung up the phone and buried her face in her hands. Twenty-five hundred dollars. Where was she going to get that kind of money for a new transmission? It would take months to save it up, provided she had a job. Which she didn't. Where would they go now? What would happen to them?

Standing, she anxiously paced around the room, her thoughts flying in a dozen directions. Maybe her mother could get a loan. She certainly couldn't. She'd sold everything she'd had to pay off the last of John's medical bills, and her credit rating was shameful.

The room grew stuffy. She needed air to breath. Hurrying out onto the deck, her gaze searched out her son playing contentedly under the trees, then to the lake moving gently against the wind. For a few short hours today, she'd found peace. A cozy cabin, a serene view, people who took care of her. But now it was all gone. She was alone and on her own again, struggling to survive.

Her knees buckled, and she sank into the rocker, scraping her fingertips along her scalp. Tears spilled onto her cheeks, and she was too overwhelmed to fight them. Drawing her knees against her chest, she lowered her head and cried.

She had only herself to blame. She'd tipped the first domino over ten years ago, and the long row had been falling at a steady pace ever since. One disaster after another. One scary event after the next. Her life was one big ball of fearful anticipation. She was tired and alone. No one to help. No one to count on. She'd pinned all her hopes on getting to her mom's, and now that was lost, too.

Now another disaster. Debt and its inevitable consequences. The phone calls, the juggling of money, the worry, the stress. She'd sworn she would never go there again. But here she was. Trapped. Not only did she owe for car repairs, but she owed Ty for staying in his cabin. Plus the food they'd eaten, her new phone and whatever else he might want to charge her for.

Closing her eyes, she thought about her mother and how easily she'd forgiven her for the years she'd ignored her parents. Her sweet forgiveness and love had lifted a cloud from her mind. Her mom had told her God had brought them together again. In the four months since they'd reconnected, Ginger had found herself slowly turning back toward her faith.

But she still found it difficult to trust the Lord completely. She had nowhere else to turn. *Oh, Lord. Please. I need help. I don't think I can do this anymore.*

Ty heard the sobbing the moment he set foot on the deck. He set the bag of groceries onto the patio table and hurried toward Ginger, who was huddled in the rocker, shoulders shaking with her weeping. He hunkered down beside her, uncertain whether to touch her or not. Her sobs were so heart-wrenching he had to risk it. He laid his hand on her arm. "What's wrong? What happened? Are you all right? Did something happen to Elliot?" He glanced quickly around and saw the boy playing happily in the yard.

"I don't know what I'm going to do. I don't know what I'm going to do."

Quickly he stood and pulled up the other rocker as close to Ginger as possible. He was at a loss to know how to proceed. He was trained to handle every kind of situation, but a weeping, incoherent female left him stumped. "Ginger. Please, tell me what happened. Maybe I can help."

She shook her head, refusing to look at him. "No one can help."

He stroked her hair, marveling at its softness and the way the waves curled around his fingers. "Okay, then. Tell me why no one can help, so I can cry with you." That got a response. She lifted her head and met his gaze. Her green eyes were swollen and red, her cheeks puffy and wet, but she looked adorable, and he fought the urge to pull her to him.

"You? Cry? Right." She lifted the edge of her long shirt, wiped at her eyes, then looked around.

"You might be surprised." He figured she was looking for a tissue, so he hurried into the house and grabbed a paper towel. What would she say if he admitted that he'd shed enough tears these past few months to fill Shiloh Lake? "Here you go."

"Thanks."

He gave her a few minutes to collect herself. "So, care to tell me what's wrong?"

She sniffed and dabbed at her nose. "They called about my car. It's going to cost over two thousand dollars to fix."

Ty exhaled a frustrated sigh. "They were supposed to call me first. I was hoping to avoid you hearing the news that way."

She shook her head. "It doesn't matter. I can't pay for it. I don't have that kind of money."

"I know. But I have a suggestion if you'll hear me out." She glanced at him, a wary look in her moist green eyes. "I talked to my mom, and we'd like to give you plane tickets to get to your mother's."

The wariness in her eyes changed instantly to lightning-laced fury. She bolted up from the chair. "No. Absolutely not."

"Why? I thought you were anxious to get to Arizona."

"I am. But not by going into debt."

"You wouldn't have to pay me back anytime soon. Never, actually."

"No. I can take care of myself. It's taken me two years to get out from under my husband's medical bills—thousands of dollars." She bit her lip. "I will never go into debt for anything or anyone again."

She wrapped one arm across her waist. The other reached up to tug on the curl at her cheek. A habit he was coming to find endearing.

"I appreciate what you're trying to do, but, no, thank you. I'll figure something out. I'll get a job. Find a place to stay. It might take me a few months to pay for the repairs, though."

"Okay." She wasn't thinking logically right now. "How do you plan on getting to and from this job if you find one?"

"I'll get a place in town. Near my work so I can walk."

"Ginger, those places are very expensive, even in a small town like Dover, and the ones close to town that you could afford aren't in the best neighborhoods."

"We're used to that." She turned and walked into the cabin, leaving him with more questions than answers. His detective instincts were raging. There was a lot more to Ginger's story than she was telling, and he wanted to know everything. How could he help her if he didn't know what he was dealing with?

He wanted to talk to her more, but maybe giving her a little space would be wiser. Remembering the groceries on the table, he went down to the car for the rest. She couldn't turn away a man with arms full of food. He'd store her belongings later.

The door to the cabin was open, so he angled his body to allow for the bags in his hands, piling them onto the island. Ginger turned and leaned against the sink, her arms crossed over her chest. "That's enough food for a year."

"I'm a growing boy. I need to eat." He pulled her new phone from his pocket. "I got you a new disposable. It was quicker. Plus this one has a few more gadgets on it. It's already activated and ready to go."

She took it slowly from his hand, as if reluctant to accept his gesture. "Thank you."

"I also brought your belongings back here. I didn't feel right leaving them in the car. We can store them in the shed below the cabin for now. That way you'll have access to them whenever you need something.

She glanced up at him, her eyes moist, her lips folded together. "I stole your bread."

"What?"

"I needed to fix Elliot lunch, so I went to your room and stole back the bread."

The guilty look on her face was comical and sweet all at the same time. He burst out laughing. The reaction surprised him because it had been many months since he'd laughed. It felt good. "It wasn't my bread. Technically, it belonged to Nels, but he gave it to you so…you're good. No arrest warrant will be issued."

A small smile moved her lips. "Thank you." She reached into a grocery bag, pulling out the jar of peanut butter and placing it in the cupboard. Ty followed her lead. Silently they worked together, putting all the food away. When he felt she was calmer, he decided to approach her again about her future.

"Ginger, don't give up hope. We'll find a solution. My family knows everyone in Dover. If you're serious about a job, we'll find one. As for a place to live, you can stay here as long as you like. Rent-free." She started to protest, but he held up his hand. "The place is paid for, and it sits empty most of the time. There's always an answer to our problems. It'll all work out." The urge to hug her overwhelmed him. Time to put some distance between himself and his lovely tenant.

"I think I'll go find Elliot and teach him how to fish. We'll be down on the pier. Take some time to clear your head." He smiled, hoping to give her some encouragement, then left the cabin. He had to find a solution, some way to help without stepping on her considerable pride. He wanted to know what had brought her to this desperate situation. But until she was ready to confide in him, there was little he could do but make himself available.

Ginger removed the chicken from the pan, placing the steamed pieces on the cutting board. With the wide variety of food Ty had purchased, she'd be able to prepare healthy meals for the next month. Tonight she'd chosen to make a simple chicken-and-noodle casserole. Quick, easy and filling. She wasn't sure how Elliot would like it, but it was time he started to broaden his taste buds. He'd be eight in just a few weeks. He was growing up so fast. She and her mother had planned on giving Elliot a big birthday party. But that probably wouldn't happen now.

Laughter and footsteps sounded at the door as Elliot and Ty entered. Elliot ran toward her, a happy smile on his face. "Mom. I caught five fish. And I caught Barney, too."

She hugged him to her side. "Barney?"

Elliot pointed to the fish on a stick that usually sat on the dresser in the fish bedroom. Elliot had brought it into the kitchen this morning. "Well, his brother anyway, but I threw him back."

Ty stopped at the end of the island. The delighted smile on his face made his blue eyes sparkle. His straight white teeth flashed against his tanned skin and deepened the creases that bracketed his mouth. She had to force herself to look away. There was something solid and dependable about Ty Durrant. Helping others seemed to come naturally to him.

"He's going to be a good fisherman. He picked it up like he was born to it. Did he and his father fish together?"

Her warm feelings faded. "No. Never."

"Mom, I have a new name. Ty gave it to me."

"Oh? You mean like a nickname?"

"Yeah. It's EJ. Isn't that cool?"

"How did you come up with that?"

"Ty asked me about my middle name, and I told him

it was Joseph, and he said EJ sounded more grown up than Elliot."

Ty wiped a hand across the side of his neck, a sheepish look on his face. "I hope that was okay."

Her heart swelled with appreciation. How could she object? He'd made her son feel special. "It's fine. Really. I'm fixing a chicken casserole for supper. You're welcome to stay."

"Thanks, but on one condition. I help with the meal."

"You cook?"

Ty grinned and walked around the counter to where the cutting board lay. "I know my way around the kitchen. Surprised?"

"Yes. I figured a bachelor like you would eat everything out of a microwave or a fast-food place."

"Guilty on all counts. At least for a while. But that got old. Mom taught each of us kids to cook the basics. Once I started experimenting, I discovered it was a great stress reliever, and I actually enjoyed it." He leaned one hip against the counter and spread his hands. "So, show me where to start."

With Ty's help, the meal was ready quickly. Elliot, who insisted he be called by his new nickname, even declared the casserole "good." High praise from her picky eater. Given the Bible she'd seen this morning, she'd expected Ty to offer a blessing, but he merely closed his eyes briefly before eating. His consideration left her feeling ashamed. Her mother had been saddened when she'd learned Ginger had ignored her faith, but John had scoffed at those who followed organized religion. It had been easier to go along with his wishes. Her greatest regret was that she'd never taken EJ to church.

Ty kept the conversation going during the meal with

bigger and more outrageous tales of his days spent at the cabin growing up. As Ginger carried the dishes to the kitchen, she tried to recall the last time she and her son had enjoyed such a happy, relaxed meal. She couldn't.

Ty came to her side and turned on the faucet, rinsing the dishes, then handing them to her to place in the dishwasher, as if cleaning up was expected of him. "You're pretty handy in the kitchen. Tomorrow night, you can cook."

He smiled at her. "Actually, tomorrow is already taken care of. I have an invitation for you. I'd like to take you and EJ to church in the morning."

His invitation caught her off guard. The thought of church filled her with anxious dread—like being called into the principal's office for misbehaving. She was still sorting through all her feelings, reaching out tentative fingers to touch the Lord again. "I couldn't impose."

"It's not an imposition."

Ginger didn't want to appear rude. Ty had done so much for them already, but she wasn't strong enough to face the Lord's disapproval yet. "We'll be fine here."

His eyes narrowed, but he didn't press the issue. "Church was only half of the invitation. You're invited to my parents' home after the service for dinner. My mother has sent her personal request. She's anxious to meet you and EJ."

"I don't know."

Ty tilted his head and smiled. "I promise you'll get a real feast. Plus, we can all put our heads together and come up with job ideas. I know EJ would love to play with my nephew, Kenny."

"Please, Mom. Ty says Kenny is fun. I want a friend to play with."

Dinner with Ty's family? Not a good idea. She had to keep her walls up. She couldn't withstand any more emotional upheaval, like making connections she'd have to sever soon. "I don't think so."

"Come on. It's only dinner."

He just didn't understand. She had to stay focused on her goal. All she wanted was to get out of Dover and to Arizona. Then she and Elliot could put the past few years behind them and start over.

"Mom?"

The excitement in her son's eyes was so wonderful to see, it weakened her resolve. Ty had a point. It was only dinner, and it would do Elliot good to have a friend to play with. "All right."

Ty and EJ exchanged fist bumps with explosions.

"Time to get ready for bed, Elliot. Go get your bath."

EJ's shoulders slumped, and he uttered a long, low groan. "A bath? Do I have to?"

His pitiful plea didn't faze her. "Yes. That means washing your hair, too."

"Mom."

"Go. You can watch television in your room for a while if you hurry. I'll even bring you some hot chocolate if you get really clean."

"TV? Really? Cool."

Ginger offered an explanation to Ty, who looked puzzled by EJ's excitement over the TV. "We haven't had a television for over a year."

Ty nodded his understanding, and leaned down to place the last plate into the dishwasher.

Ginger noticed him wince, her gaze landing on his neck and the ugly scar that ran along the side, ending near his collarbone. She sucked in sharply. "Ty? What happened to you?"

He froze in place, then slowly straightened, a strange, forced smile on his face. "I didn't duck fast enough."

His flippant remark sparked anger. "What?"

"I was shot."

Her heart stopped beating. Memories flared. "Why? What happened?"

"My partner and I were caught in an ambush. He died. I took three rounds."

Her brain was processing the information in slow motion. "Partner?"

"I'm a detective with the Dallas P.D. I'm on medical leave. Recuperating."

"You're a policeman?" Her mind recoiled with the knowledge. A man who carried a gun. A man who lived a life of violence. Always in harm's way. Always on the edge of death. She turned away from him, leaning against the side of the fridge. This couldn't be happening again.

"Ginger, what's wrong? Are you all right?"

She shook her head. "I can't believe this. I thought I could get away from the violence and the danger. All I wanted was to put that behind me."

"Put what behind you? You're not making any sense." He came toward her, but she ducked into the living room.

"Of course I'm not making any sense. None of it makes sense. I've been over it a million times, relived every moment in my head, but there's still no rhyme or reason for any of it." Suddenly drained, she sank down onto the hearth, one hand covering her mouth. Ty sat on the coffee table, his eyes filled with concern. For her. It had been a long time since anyone had looked at her that way. As if she mattered.

Her gaze drifted from the questions in his eyes to the side of his neck and the ugly scar. She shuddered as a wave of terror and helplessness tore through her. "My husband was shot. We stopped at a fast-food restaurant one night. Elliot wanted one of their kids' meals. We were in a hurry, so John ran in to get the food. He brought the food out, then went back inside. They'd given him the wrong change. I heard the shots. I… Two people were killed. John was shot in the back. He was paralyzed from the waist down. He was a security guard. The police later speculated that when he went back in he was probably mistaken for a real policeman, and the shooter panicked."

Ty bowed his head, then looked up at her. His hand slipped over hers, his fingers closing around hers gently. "I'm so sorry. I had no idea. And Elliot?"

"He didn't see anything. But he heard the shots." She wanted to pull her hand from Ty's, but the warmth of his touch gave her comfort. It was nice to have someone to listen, someone who would actually understand. There'd been no one to share her fear with, her heartache. "That day changed everything. One act of senseless violence. One stupid gunman. I've tried to understand and make sense of it, but I can't."

"There's no sense to it."

"I never understood why he liked the job or why the uniform made him feel so invincible. He was only a security guard at an office building. He signed people in and out, but he liked carrying that gun." She looked up at him. "Why do you do it? Why do you choose to live a life filled with violence?"

Ty's blue eyes darkened to gray. "I didn't. I was called to a job where I could stand in the gap between people like you and the ones who commit the violence."

"But the violence touched you."

"True." He inhaled a slow breath. "I don't have any easy answers for you, Ginger. I don't have answers for myself right now."

The same conclusions she'd come to. No answers. No explanation. No closure. She pulled her fingers from Ty's grasp. "I'm tired. I'm going to bed." She stood, folding her arms across her chest. "Thank you for helping with supper."

Ty stood and nodded. "Okay. Are you still coming to my parents' tomorrow? I think you'll enjoy it."

"I don't know. I'm too tired to think about it. Good night."

Ginger heard the door click behind him, watching as he walked across the deck and disappeared around the corner. Ty was a cop. The last man on earth she wanted to be dependent on. So why did she want to call him back and hold his hand again?

With a huff, she headed for the bedroom. Because she was alone again and feeling vulnerable. Well, she'd been there before, and she'd get through this crisis, too. And she'd do it all by herself.

Chapter Four

No answers. Not for him or for Ginger. The look in her green eyes when she'd learned he was a cop burned into his memory, and stirred an old sadness. She'd never look at him the same way again. He couldn't blame her. After what she'd experienced. Her situation only pointed up why he'd never married. No wife should have to live with that kind of fear or that kind of tragedy.

He rolled over, making the old bed groan and creak in protest. Her fingers had felt so delicate and small in his hand. He'd felt them tremble as she'd told her story. He wanted to pull her into his arms and hold her close, chase the fear away and reassure her that she was safe.

There was something special about Ginger Sloan. She'd gotten under his skin. She reminded him of the magnolia trees that stood on the property. Strong. Graceful. Her eyes were the same dark green as the shiny leaves. Her creamy complexion rivaled the white flowers with their flawless petals. Her dark auburn hair had streaks of the cinnamon color of the underside of the leaves, soft and rich. She was strong, beautiful and brave.

Enduring. Somehow she'd managed to overcome the adversity in her life all alone.

But she was filled with fear, and she didn't have to be if she'd only allow the Lord to carry her burdens. It didn't take much to see that her troubles had caused a crisis in her faith. Maybe he could help her see that the Lord was on her side, not against her. He stretched out on his back, sending up a prayer for her comfort as he drifted off to sleep.

Gunshots.

Ty sat up in bed, searching the darkness for an intruder. He was alone. In the boathouse. Dragging a shaking hand over his damp face, he sucked in a few calming breaths. Nightmare. He lay back down, staring at the ceiling. It had been weeks since he'd had one. He'd hoped he'd finally gotten past that part. This one had been different. A new image had appeared. The men with guns were still there, appearing out of nowhere, firing at him. He'd felt the impact as the bullets had seared his body. Seen Pete lying on the ground, but this time, Ginger and EJ had been there, and the gun had been trained on them. He'd tried to warn them, to place himself in front of the gunman, but he hadn't been able to move—hadn't been able to force sounds from his throat. He'd seen the bullet leave the barrel—and then he'd awakened.

He couldn't continue like this. Living with the questions. The doubt. The guilt. He needed answers, and he was tired of waiting for the Lord to shine a light on his path.

Ginger hugged the warm cup of coffee between her palms, staring into the empty fireplace replaying once again the scene from last night. Ty had been shot. In the line of duty. Duty as a cop. Her dreams had been rife with frightening images of guns and policemen, and John smiling in his uniform. But when she'd looked closer, it hadn't been her husband but Ty, his hand to his neck, falling to the ground.

She blinked the images away. She'd learned the hard way that dwelling on those thoughts only made things worse and plunged her mood into a dark place. When she and Elliot had set out on their journey to her mother in Arizona, she'd vowed to bury those memories forever and never look at them again. It had worked until she'd landed here at Shiloh Lake in a cabin owned by a wounded cop. A very handsome and kind cop. She was tempted to accept his offer of plane tickets. Fly to Mom's and cut her losses. If the job her mom mentioned was a sure thing, she would take him up on his offer. But it wasn't. It was only the promise of an interview. But Ty's offer meant going into debt again. Pride was all she had left at the moment. Besides, it was an emotion she understood. Either she took Ty's offer and went further in debt to him, or she stayed and battled her own way out of this mess. Battling was something she understood. Indebtedness was a place she never wanted to revisit.

She stood and moved to the kitchen to refill her cup, but a knock on the cabin door turned her around. Ty. Through the glass panes she had a clear view, and the sight made her mouth suddenly dry. He was dressed in a suit and tie, ready for church. The perfectly fitted dark gray jacket emphasized his broad shoulders, and the crisp white shirt brought out his tanned skin. She opened the door, putting a smile on her face. He really was easy on the eyes. "Coffee is ready."

He didn't smile back. Her throat tightened. He looked serious, his blue eyes dark, his mouth held in a firm line.

"No, thanks. I'll grab some at church. I just wanted to see if you and EJ are still coming with me to my folks for dinner."

She inhaled a deep breath, then wished she hadn't because she breathed in the tangy scent of his aftershave. This was a different side of him. Clean-shaven, hair damp and combed neatly to one side. It grazed the edges of his collar in the back and waved slightly over his forehead. She had a sudden desire to brush it back and test the feel of it.

Dinner. She had struggled all night with that question, alternating between wanting to go and wanting to hide in the cabin. "Well, I…"

"Ty!" Elliot darted around her and stopped, staring up at Ty.

"Hey, EJ."

Ty's grim expression dissolved when he looked at Elliot. His blue eyes sparked, his smile widened and softened the edges of his mouth. The transformation was heart-stopping.

"I have a special name for you, Ty," Elliot blurted out excitedly. "I made it up myself."

"Well, let's hear it."

"The Tyster." Elliot fairly bounced with pride.

Ty raised his hand to his chin, rubbing it thoughtfully as if considering the new nickname.

"Tyster. I like it. Tyster and EJ. We sound like superheroes." He exchanged fist bumps with the boy.

Ginger's heart nearly burst from her chest. In the short time they'd known Ty Durrant, he'd paid more attention to Elliot than his own father ever had.

Ty looked at her, his blue eyes probing. His expression serious again. "So are you coming?"

How could she refuse now? "All right."

"I'll come back and pick you up after the service. Dress casual. We're not a fancy family."

She nodded, wishing he'd smile at her again. His smile had sent a ray of warmth over her like stepping from a dark forest into the sunlight. "Okay. We'll be ready."

"Bye, Tyster."

Ty waved and walked across the deck toward the stairs. Elliot ran to the window and watched him until he disappeared around the corner. "Mom, we're superheroes."

Ginger and Elliot were ready and waiting when she heard Ty's car pull in below the cabin later that morning. She'd changed her clothes three times, finally deciding to take him at his word and wear her dark jeans and a plain gold V-neck sweater. She added a pair of small heart-shaped earrings as a final touch.

When Ty didn't appear at the door, she stepped out onto the deck in time to see him walking toward the boathouse. Probably to change clothes. He walked with an easy, confident gait, broad shoulders dipping and rolling as he moved, his long stride chewing up the yard. His arms swung easily at his side. He walked with authority. The authority of a police officer. It didn't take much imagination to envision him with a badge on his belt and a holster at his side.

Her heart made an extra beat in her chest. Ty was an attractive and compelling man, and he made her aware every moment that she was a woman. But he was a cop. A man who carried a gun and put his life on the line every single day. When he disappeared into the boathouse, she went back inside to gather her things. She and Elliot were waiting at the top of the cabin steps when he returned. Elliot darted down the steps to greet him. "Tyster."

Ty gave him a friendly head rub, then unlocked the car. Once safely belted inside the luxurious SUV, Ginger allowed her son's chatter to fill the space. It was easier than trying to talk. She sensed Ty was in a bad mood, probably because of her outburst last night.

The ride was taking more time than she expected, and it dawned on her just how far out of town the lake cabins were. It would have been better if she'd gone to church with him and saved him the long drive.

The country road soon gave way to a three-lane highway. Stores and businesses started to appear. Ty slowed for the railroad track, and when he crossed over, the landscape changed. Two brick pillars bracketed a large sign. *Welcome to Dover.* She smiled as they passed through the charming downtown area. It was the quintessential nineteenth-century small town. Built around a center square with majestic courthouse and brick buildings lining the streets.

"Oh, look at the gazebo. How lovely."

Ty nodded. "It is now. Thanks to my sister, Laura."

Ginger turned to him for an explanation.

"A couple months ago some guy crashed his car into it, and he and my sister, the contractor, had to restore it. She's marrying the guy in a few weeks."

"Oh?"

Ty shook his head. "I don't know all the details. I haven't even met him yet."

As they passed out of the downtown area, Ginger found herself wishing she could explore the little shops and stores. It had been a long time since she'd had the luxury of simply enjoying her surroundings. If she found a job here, she'd be able to do that.

The streets on this side of Dover were lined with huge Victorian homes and brick mansions. Ty made a left turn onto another tree-lined street, only to slow at the sight of two cars up against each other. Steam rose from the hood of one. The drivers stood face-to-face, gesturing wildly, obviously upset. He slowed and pulled up to the curb. He released the seat belt and started to get out of the car.

"Where are you going?"

"To see if I can help. Stay here."

She reached for his arm to stop him, but he was already out of the car and moving quickly toward the drivers. Concern for his safety increased her heartbeat. He didn't need to get involved. She saw him stride forward, but a few feet shy of the men, he stopped.

"Where's Tyster going, Mom?"

"He's checking to see if everyone is okay."

"Why?"

Might as well deal with the inevitable. "Because Ty's a policeman, Elliot."

"Really? Way cool."

Her heart sank. She did not want her son entertaining ideas about becoming a cop. She watched as Ty spoke to the men, one of whom looked extremely upset. He was waving his hands in the air and pointing at the other driver. Ty nodded a few times, then glanced over his shoulder. A patrol car was pulling up. Once the officer was out of the vehicle, Ty returned to the car, sliding in behind the wheel and quickly pulling his seat belt across his chest, snapping it in place.

"Sorry about that. Turned out to be nothing real serious. Just a lot of crunched-up metal and some angry drivers."

"Tyster, Mom says you're a policeman."

Ty gave her an understanding glance before replying, "Yes, I am. A hungry one. Let's get to my parents' place so we can eat."

"And meet Kenny."

He nodded, then turned the key in the ignition. His hand shook as he took the wheel, alarming Ginger. "Are you all right?"

He glanced at her before engaging the transmission. "What?"

She reached over and lightly touched his hand. "You're shaking."

He gripped the wheel. "It's nothing."

His tone told her it was definitely something. She sensed a change in his mood. And there was a tension in his shoulders that hadn't been there before.

Soon they turned down a street in an old, established neighborhood with large trees and charming homes, rich with character. Ty pulled the car to a stop in front of a two-story white house, plucked from her deepest dreams. From the twin dormers on its roof and the abundance of mullioned windows to the wide, welcoming front porch, it was the image of a family home. She climbed out of the car, unable to pull her gaze from the stately home. "Ty, this is beautiful. Did you grow up here?"

"For the most part. I was ten when we moved."

She took Elliot's hand. If the inside was as lovely as the outside, she'd have to watch him every moment. She could not afford to replace anything he might break.

Ty opened the beveled glass front door, stepping to one side to allow her and Elliot to enter the foyer.

The inside met her expectations. Warm and welcoming, it was filled with traditional furnishings, lovingly worn by years of use. Her parents had favored a stark contemporary style. Growing up, she'd ached for something warm and homey. Something exactly like this. She caught a glimpse of an office to one side and a formal living room on the other. A broad staircase rose to the second floor across from a formal dining room.

An uneasy sensation began in the pit of her stomach, a mixture of insecurity and fear at meeting his family. She turned to look at Ty for some reassurance, only to find his expression tight and closed off. A deep scowl creased his forehead. His shoulders were braced with tension.

Before she could ask him what was wrong, a pretty blonde stepped in front of them, a huge smile on her face. She made a beeline for Ty, squealing as she wrapped her arms around his neck.

"There you are. It's so good to see you. I've missed you."

"Me, too, sis."

Ginger saw Ty's tension ease somewhat, but the smile he offered his sister was lacking real warmth. Ginger's tension spiked. Maybe he'd lied about his family situation.

"You must be Ginger. I'm Laura Durrant, Ty's baby sister. We're so glad you came today. And this must be Elliot." She turned and shouted over her shoulder. "Kenny, Elliot is here."

Ty steered them toward the back of the house into the kitchen, where a wave of shouts and expressions of joy rose up as everyone welcomed Ty back into the family. Ginger pulled Elliot to her side, stepping back to allow the reunion to go unimpeded. She couldn't help but smile at the loving welcome he received. She always dreamed of a family like this. Brothers, sisters, cousins.

She tried to sort out the people as she watched. The older woman with short, graying blond hair must be his mother. Two tall, dark, attractive men stood together near the back door. The first one shook Ty's hand, then yanked him into a brotherly hug, a huge smile on his handsome face. The older brother, Matt. The other man extended his hand and smiled. Ty shook the man's hand, but Ginger noticed his back straightened.

"I'm so sorry we're ignoring you. I'm Angie Durrant, Ty's mother."

"Ginger Sloan, and this is my son, Elliot."

"We're so glad you came. Let me introduce you to everyone. We're all a bit overwhelmed. This is the first time Ty has been home since he— In several months." She stopped and placed a hand to her throat, looking into Ginger's eyes. "We almost lost him, you know."

A shaft of fear raced along her nerves. She'd seen Ty's scar, but she hadn't allowed herself to wonder about the details of the shooting. Now she couldn't help but look at Ty and worry.

Angie took her arm, guiding her to the opening between the family room and the kitchen, which seemed to be where everyone congregated. Ginger smiled as she met older brother, Matt, and his new wife, Shelby. Laura returned with her fiancé in tow, Adam Holbrook, an attractive man with piercing green eyes who was obviously in love with Ty's sister.

"Don't forget me."

A girl about twelve pushed between her parents. "I'm Cassidy."

"Nice to meet you. This is…" She looked for her son.

He was standing in the kitchen, showing his favorite car to a boy about his age. The pair looked as if they'd been friends forever. It was good to see Elliot coming out of his shell. It had been a difficult and lonely couple of years for him. She smiled at Cassidy. "That's Elliot, and I'm guessing that's Kenny."

Laura perched on one of the stools at the kitchen island, her friendly, easy manner calming the butterflies in Ginger's stomach. She was a lovely, petite woman; her thick dark blond hair flowed in expertly cut layers around her face. She was dressed in faded jeans and a layered top Ginger had seen in magazines, but would have no idea how to wear. From her platform shoes to the stylish earrings, she looked pulled together and confident. Something Ginger never felt. Smoothing the front of her simple sweater, she scolded herself for making comparisons.

Laura shifted on the stool, leaning toward her. "So, I hear you're looking for a job."

Ty had mentioned he'd speak with his family about her situation, but she hadn't anticipated what that would mean. "Um, yes. My car needs work, and I'll have to find a job to pay for the repairs."

"What kind of work are you looking for?"

"Anything. Waiting tables, flipping burgers." She laughed lightly in an attempt to brush off the embarrassment. Ty had told her about his sister's company. Laura was a successful businesswoman. Ginger was homeless and desperate for any job she could find. "For the last few years I've worked as the assistant director of a parks department in Connecticut."

Laura's eyes lit up. "Really. Wow. I wish you were staying here longer. I have a position coming up you'd be perfect for. I'm opening a senior center downtown, and I'll need a director to run things. But, unfortunately, we've only just started the renovations, and it'll be summer before I need to fill that spot."

Shelby Durrant slid into the stool on her other side, making Ginger feel like the country mouse sandwiched between two city mice. A little taller than Laura, Shelby was slender and elegant, her dark brown hair pulled into a long braid at the back of her head. From the tips of her suede high-heeled boots to the leggings beneath a flowing shirt wrapped with an ornate belt that showed off her tiny waist to the large dangling earrings, she looked as if she'd stepped from the pages of a New York fashion magazine.

Shelby sighed and lightly touched her hand. "I wish I could help. I'm starting a small business soon, but I haven't even finalized the lease on the space yet, or I'd hire you in a minute."

"Thank you. I'm sure something will turn up."

Her gaze traveled to Ty, who was standing in the middle of the family room, talking to his father. Mr. Durrant had his back to her, but she could clearly see Ty's face, and it was obvious he wasn't happy. His mouth was in a tight line as his father pointed and gestured, obviously trying to convey some important information.

Ginger had the strangest urge to rescue him. Ty caught her gaze and smiled, then steered his father toward her. He was the only person she hadn't met yet. She angled the stool to face Ty and his dad as they joined her at the kitchen island.

"Ginger Sloan, this is my father, Tom Durrant. Dad. Ginger."

The elder Durrant's smile was as dazzling and charming as his youngest son's. He shook her hand. "I'm delighted to meet you. I hear you're staying at Ty's cabin."

"Yes, he's been very generous about letting us stay there."

"Well, if he gives you any trouble, you let me know." He softened his words with a wink and broad smile.

"Dad." Ty shifted his weight and rubbed his neck.

"I'll do that." She smiled at Ty, who held her gaze, bringing a warmth into her cheeks. Quickly she turned her attention to his dad. Mr. Durrant was an older version of his son Matt. Ty and Laura seemed to favor their mother in looks and coloring, though it wasn't hard to see the family resemblance between the three children. The men were all around six feet tall, broad-shouldered with long legs, but where Matt and his dad were more solidly built, Ty was lean, sleek and elegant. And Laura was a younger version of her mother.

Dinner was delicious, and Ginger found herself content to sit and watch the family interact. They prayed over the meal together, laughed, argued and eventually tossed around ideas for her future employment.

"Too bad I don't need anyone at the hardware store, but between Adam and myself, we're doing great."

Ginger felt Ty stiffen beside her. "Thank you all for your help. I appreciate it."

After the meal Ginger went to check on Elliot and Kenny, who'd disappeared the moment their food was finished. She found them in the corner of the front room surrounded by toys. The place was a mess. She started to tell Elliot to pick up, but Angie Durrant touched her shoulder.

"Don't worry about that. I like seeing the mess. It reminds me of when the kids were little. Sometimes I leave it there for a day or so, just remembering."

The sweet sentiment touched her. What she wouldn't give for a family like this, people to surround her, support her, love her and not judge. Unlike Laura and Shelby, she had no career aspirations. All she'd ever wanted was a family, a home of her own, someone to love her. She turned to speak to Mrs. Durrant when she saw something she'd completely missed before. In the bay window of the large room stood a black baby grand piano. "What a lovely instrument."

"Do you play?"

Ginger nodded, touching the gleaming white keys with her fingertips and lightly pressing down on a key. "I used to. I took lessons for years. I was studying music in college, but then I got married." She shrugged. No need to reflect on that.

"You're welcome to play this one anytime you want. Laura took lessons for a long time. Ty and Matt, too, though neither one of them kept up with it once they started playing sports. Well, I think it's time I cut the cake. Three-layer chocolate with chocolate fudge icing. Ty's favorite."

Ginger lingered at the piano for a few minutes, allowing the warm and comfortable sensations of the gathering to seep into her bones. She wanted to make a permanent mental snapshot of the day to treasure. It had been nearly perfect. Elliot had made a new friend, the Durrants had treated her like one of their own, and she'd had the opportunity to live her dream for one day.

The only sour note was Ty. He'd been quiet and withdrawn, bordering on surly the entire time, and she wasn't sure why. As if hearing her thoughts, Ty strode through the foyer and out the front door.

Chapter Five

Ty strode to the edge of the front porch, sucking the cool, damp air into his lungs, allowing the bracing air to settle his nerves and clear his head. Leaning against the post, he wrapped an arm around it, resting the other on his hip as he fought to master his anger. Dad wanted him to take over a church project while he was here. Why couldn't he understand that was the last thing he wanted to do? He needed time to think, not do busy work.

He'd wanted this visit with his family to be enjoyable for Ginger and EJ. Instead, he'd arrived sullen and defensive. He never should have stopped to help with the car accident. The simple gesture had triggered an anxiety attack, calling up all his doubts about his ability to remain in law enforcement. What if one of the men had been armed? What if they'd come to blows? Would he have had the courage and strength to handle the situation? Or would he have cowered from the danger and run away? The idea sickened him. The worst part was, no one could understand his struggle.

"Ty. Are you all right?"

He jerked around. The concern in Ginger's dark gaze

touched him. "Fine. Just needed some air, that's all." He forced a small smile. "Are you feeling overwhelmed? Our family has grown suddenly. Lots more people. More noise."

"I loved every minute of it. Your family is wonderful."

He nodded. They were wonderful, but he didn't need the well-meaning hugs and words from family right now. He needed space and time to sort out his life.

Ginger moved to his side, laying her small hand on his arm. "If you'd like to leave, we can. I'll tell them Elliot is tired and needs to get to sleep or something."

Her consideration warmed him. He thought back to what she'd told him about her husband. She was probably the only person he knew who might really understand some of what he was dealing with. He had an overwhelming urge to tell her his deepest secrets. "You wouldn't mind? We haven't had dessert yet."

"We'll take some home with us."

A stiff, damp breeze blew across the porch. Ty glanced at the rapidly darkening sky. "I think I have a more logical excuse." He turned and took her arm, leading her back inside. When they reached the kitchen, Ty announced that they were leaving because of the bad storm forecast for the evening. No one questioned his decision.

After making their goodbyes and collecting enough cake to last two days, they made their escape. They rode in silence through downtown Dover, the skies growing more ugly by the moment. Ty could sense Ginger's curious gaze watching him, trying to figure out what was bothering him. She broke the silence as they crossed the railroad tracks.

"I like your family."

"I'm glad. They're pretty great." He eased the car to a

stop at the traffic light. "They liked you, too." He'd been pleased at how easily she'd fit in.

"Laura invited me to her wedding. If I'm still here, that is."

Ty exhaled a sigh and shook his head. "Yeah."

"You don't approve? Adam obviously loves your sister."

"I suppose. He seems decent enough." He rubbed his forehead. "So much has changed since I was home last. My brother remarried, my sister is engaged to a guy who's buying the family business and taking over and my parents are retiring and thinking about moving away. It's a lot to adjust to."

"You were looking for the old familiar dynamic, and it's not there anymore."

Ty stole a quick glance at her. She'd put into words the emotions he hadn't been able to identify. "Yeah, I guess." Inwardly he flinched at his tone. He sounded like a pouty child.

"Your mother offered to let Elliot and me stay at the house."

"I'm not surprised. She loves taking care of people. What did you tell her?"

"Thank you, but no thank you."

"Really? Why?"

"I love your parents' home. It's what I've always longed for, but I like the quiet at the cabin. I'd like to stay there."

For some reason her words filled him with warmth. "My mom offered me the same deal. She said I could come home and stay in my old room."

Ginger laughed lightly. "It would be more comfortable than that little shack you stay in."

"Maybe, but I turned her down. I like the atmosphere at the lake. Always have."

A mischievous twinkle lit Ginger's eyes. "I won't tell if you won't."

"Deal."

Ginger stood at the large windows at the front of the cabin. The skies had opened up, sending drenching rain and slanting winds across the lake, and buffeting the raised cabin. She shivered and turned back to the kitchen, where Ty and EJ—she was growing fond of that nickname—were inspecting a row of toy cars.

A sudden fierce clap of thunder pulled a sharp squeal from her throat. Ty spun around to look at her. "You okay?"

"Yes. It's a really bad storm. They just issued a tornado watch. But it's winter."

"Yeah, I saw that. It's on the far side of the lake moving northeast. We're on the southern edge here, so we should be fine. Tornados aren't common this time of year, but they do happen. We'll keep a close eye on it. I've already collected flashlights and some candles. The weather radio has fresh batteries, so you'll be all right. If things get too bad, we'll go back to my parents." He looked at her. "Maybe we both should have taken Mom up on her offer."

She looked at his easy smile, his calm demeanor and the solid mass of him. He gave her a sense of safety. "Ty, if you wouldn't mind, could you stay here with us until the storm passes?"

A slow smiled lifted one corner of his mouth. "Hadn't planned on leaving. I'll stretch out on the couch later. You can lock the bedroom doors."

She shook her head. "I trust you." Surprisingly, she did.

The storm continued through the evening with no signs of letting up. Fortunately, they didn't lose power, passing the time with a movie and playing a board game. Later, Ty roughhoused with Elliot, eliciting squeals of delight. Together, they fixed soup and sandwiches for supper, then served up the cake from his mother's for dessert. Whatever had been bothering him earlier had disappeared.

When Elliot had been sent to bed, Ginger poured a fresh cup of coffee and joined Ty on the sofa. He'd tuned the television to the Weather Network to keep track of the storm, which would last several more hours.

Ginger sipped her coffee, enjoying the warmth of the fire Ty had built. With the storm raging outside, she welcomed the security and protection inside the cabin, but it also made her acutely aware of Ty's very male presence. Knowing Ty would be spending the night with them filled her with conflicting emotions. She welcomed his company as a safety net from the storm, but having him in the cabin all night also made her uncomfortable.

He, on the other hand, seemed very comfortable here. But then, why wouldn't he? It was his home. She was the one who should feel awkward. But she didn't. The little cabin had quickly become her sanctuary, the first place she'd felt safe and secure in a long time. Her thoughts turned to her mother, creating an overwhelming need to hear her voice. On the excuse of wanting to check in on EJ, she rose and started from the room.

"Ginger, see if you can sneak that fish out of EJ's room. I want to have a little fun with him."

"All right." Back in her room, she pulled out her cell and dialed her mother.

"Ginger. Are you okay? I'm watching the weather, and it looks really bad over there."

"We're fine, Mom. The cabin is strong, and we're not alone."

"Oh? Who's with you?"

The question stumped her. How did she explain Ty? Landlord? Friend? Cop? The man she was strongly attracted to? "The owner is here. He's going to hang around until the storm passes. We'll be fine, Mom."

"I want you back to me safe and sound, sweetheart. It's been so long, and I've missed you so much. I've prayed for you every day since you left."

"I know."

The words lodged in her heart, but instead of delivering the sting it normally did, it brought her a sense of comfort and gratitude. How could her mother pray for a daughter who had turned her back on the values she'd been raised with and the dreams her parents had for her? She thought about EJ and suddenly understood that a mother's love didn't change or fade if the child rebelled. "I love you, Mom. We'll get there as soon as I can, I promise."

"Ginny, honey, try and let go of the fear. Give the Lord a chance to help you."

"I'm trying."

Wiping tears from her eyes, she slipped the phone in her pocket and started back to the living area, but first she quietly opened EJ's door and lifted the fish from the dresser. She handed it to Ty, who had moved the side chairs closer to the roaring fire, his feet propped up on the hearth. "What are you going to do with it?"

He smiled a little-boy smile. "The same thing my uncle Dale did when I used to stay here." He stood and placed Barney on the island, then he pulled out a box of cereal and sprinkled a handful of flakes at the base of the fish. Next, he took a few cake crumbs from the plate and added them to the mix. Ginger saw what he was doing and giggled.

Ty stood back to admire his handiwork. "Barney has been a naughty little fish."

"Did your uncle do this all the time?"

He refilled his coffee cup, then returned to the chairs in front of the fire. "Yep. I never knew where Barney would be in the morning. It was always a treat to wake up and see what he'd been up to."

"EJ will love this. You're good with kids, Ty. You should have some of your own."

He fingered his cup, staring into the dark liquid. "Yeah, well, that's not on the radar right now. How's your mom?"

"Worried. Missing us, and anxious to meet her grandson."

"You sure you won't take me up on the offer of a plane ticket?"

"No. But thank you." She sat down and propped her feet on the hearth beside Ty's. The image created a longing in her heart. How nice it would be to have someone to curl up with each night and discuss the day's events. She'd never had that with John. Her throat tightened. The mixture of emotions stirred up today slammed into her, leaving behind an aching loneliness. She wanted a normal life—someone to hold her, take care of her for a change. "My mom has been praying for me." The tears threatened. She wasn't sure why she'd told him that.

"That's what moms do." His deep voice was thick with compassion.

"But I disowned them. I didn't speak to them for nearly ten years."

"Care to tell me why?"

What would it hurt? "My parents were much older when they had me, so I grew up around adults. I always felt out of step with the kids in my class. I never understood their music or their obsession with boys and clothes and makeup. I hated being different and weird. I wanted to be like everyone else. So when I went to collage I rebelled. I didn't call home, didn't visit. I was free, and I intended to experience everything they'd warned me about."

"How did that work out?"

She drew her feet up under her. "Not good. I met John. He was in a band on campus. I was studying music, so we hit it off. He was going to be this big success, and I was going to be his manager. Only I had no idea how to do that. The band eventually fell apart, but by then we were married. He managed to get enough gigs to keep food on the table, but when I got pregnant, he agreed to settle down and find a job. Only John wasn't cut out for the nine-to-five life, and I ended up being the provider."

"What about Elliot?"

"John loved him, but he never knew what to do with him." She took a sip of her coffee, her tension easing. It felt good to talk to someone about things she'd kept to herself for so long. "After the shooting, John had a hard time adjusting to his situation. He became angry and bitter. We'd managed to buy a little house a few years earlier, but the medical bills kept mounting, and we finally had to sell it. He developed complications, mainly because he refused to do what the doctors told him. After he died, I tried to pay off the bills. I even took a cheap apartment to cut our expenses, but that was a mistake. Some men broke into our apartment one night."

"Ginger." Ty shifted in his chair to face her. "Were you hurt?"

She shook her head. "They ran out when they saw us. I guess they thought the apartment was empty. But it was just one more thing to be afraid of. The last straw was losing my job. Finally I swallowed my pride and called my mom. She told me to come home. I sold what was left, paid off the last hospital bill and started for Arizona." Ginger kept her gaze on the crackling fire. What would Ty think of her pitiful tale? Would he think her a coward or just too weak to face her mistakes? "So now you know the whole story. I just want to get to a safe place. Away from guns and shootings and catastrophes around every corner."

"So that's why you were so upset to learn I was a cop?"

She nodded. "A gun destroyed my life. Everything changed. Especially John. He turned into someone I didn't know anymore."

Ty stood, placing one foot on the hearth, his left arm resting on the mantel. "Personality change is common after an accident. When I was a junior in high school, my dad was in a bad car accident. He suffered multiple injuries, several surgeries. He became a totally different person for a while. We didn't understand it. He was angry and short-tempered. Sometimes he'd withdraw and not speak to anyone. It was hard."

"Elliot didn't understand. He was only five. It frightened him. He became shy and fearful." She looked over at him. "I appreciate you paying attention to him—treating him like a normal little boy. He's missed that."

"He's a great kid. I like his enthusiasm. I think he'll…"

An ear-piercing crack exploded outside. Ginger froze. "What was that?"

Ty hurried to the window. "Lightning strike and it was close." He moved to the door, grabbed his hooded sweatshirt and went outside to the deck, returning quickly with his cell in his hand. "Looks like a cabin down the way has been hit. I'm going to check it out."

Ty had placed a call to the fire department before it registered in her mind what he was going to do. "No, you should stay here. It's dangerous out there in the storm," Ginger warned.

"I've got to go, Ginger. Someone might need help."

The old, gnawing fear spiraled up from her core. "You've called the fire department. I'm sure they'll be here quickly."

"We're ten miles from town. It might be too late. I'll come back as soon as they get here. It'll be fine."

She was unable to look at him. That's what John had said to her each time he'd left for work in that stupid uniform. She turned back in time to see the door close behind him, his shadowed form passing in front of the windows before disappearing.

Unable to move, she stared at the window. Rain poured down the panes and pounded on the roof. Thunder boomed. She moved to the chair, casting her gaze toward the television. The sound was muted, but the information displayed on the screen told her all she needed to know. Severe storm warning. Dangerous lighting. Hurricane force winds. Possible hail. The tornado may have bypassed them, but the storm was still a threat.

What if Ty got injured trying to help someone in the fire? Why did men always have to be the hero? Superheroes, that's what he'd told EJ they were. That's what he was. To her. He'd stepped in and held out a lifeline. But what if he died?

An icy chill surged through her veins. She could never do this again—the waiting, the worrying, the uncertainty. She was already feeling a connection with Ty, but that was a mistake. She needed safety, and he wasn't a safe kind of guy.

She had to stop this. It was pointless. And absurd. Ty was only an acquaintance. Nothing more. Wasn't he?

She paced to the door and looked out. The rain was coming down sideways, so hard she couldn't see a thing. Overhead the thunder rumbled continuously, shaking the raised cabin. A quick check on Elliot found him sound asleep. In the living area, she tried to calm down by looking at the fire. No sooner had she propped her feet up on the hearth than the power went out. A new fear crawled up her spine.

Spying the LED lantern Ty had placed on the hearth earlier, she lifted it and found the switch, the light chasing away some of her tension. Her gaze traveled to the clock on the mantel. Ty had only been gone twenty minutes. She hadn't heard a siren, which meant the fire department hadn't arrived yet.

Pulling her knees up to her chest, she lowered her head and prayed.

The rain refused to slacken as Ty trudged up the stairs of his cabin and crossed to the door. He inhaled, but the acrid smoke from the burning cabin still stung his nostrils and made him cough. He should have taken Ginger's advice and stayed with her. He'd been little use at his neighbors'. He'd charged in like he always did, ready to help and handle the situation, but when he'd arrived, the fear had slammed into him, bringing with it the guilt and the doubt.

The owners had made it out on their own, safe and sound, and the fire department had been notified. The cabin was burning rapidly, even with the pouring rain. The boom and roll of thunder had triggered memories of the shooting, so instead of taking charge, he'd pulled back, battling his inner doubts.

He hesitated, with his hand on the doorknob, as a new thought filled his mind. Maybe his reaction tonight was God's way of telling him he wasn't cut out for the job anymore. Time to turn in the badge and walk away. But if it was, why did his heart ache at the thought?

He stepped inside the cabin, pulling off the rain poncho he'd grabbed from his car on the way out. Even with it, he'd ended up soaked through.

"Ty!"

Ginger flew toward him, her deep green eyes wide with worry. She stopped only inches away, her gaze raking him up and down.

"Are you all right?"

Words stuck in his throat. How did he answer that? "Yeah. I'm fine."

Suddenly she was wrapped around him, her arms hugging his neck, her body pressed against him. He slid his hands to her back, holding on. Somewhere deep inside he felt a seismic shift, a tilting of his once solid and level foundation.

"I was so worried."

"Nothing to worry about. Everyone was out before I got there, but the cabin is probably a total loss." He expected her to release him, but she clung to him tightly. He realized there was more to her welcome than simple relief. A finger of concern traced along his spine. "Ginger. It's okay. Really."

"I was afraid you wouldn't come back."

He thought about what she'd told him about her husband. He knew well the knee-jerk reaction to old fear. Now, holding Ginger in his arms, he wished he could tell her about his scars, about the guilt. Maybe she would understand. "You can't get rid of me that easily."

She pulled back then, her gaze locking with his. "But you're my only friend here in town. I don't know what I'd do without you."

His heart beat erratically for a moment. "Are we friends?" He realized with a jolt that he wanted her as a friend, and maybe more. The thought scared him.

Ginger's expression suddenly changed, and she slipped her hands from his shoulders where they had been resting. "Of course we're friends."

She smiled, but Ty saw the wariness behind her pretty eyes. She took another step back and examined him. "Ty, you're soaking wet. You need to get out of those clothes. I don't have anything to give you."

Ty shook his head. "I have some clothes I keep here. The bottom drawer of the dresser in the master bedroom."

She waved him on. "Go. Get what you need."

"How long has the power been out?" He picked up the LED lantern.

"About ten minutes, I guess."

Ty moved down the hallway, his emotions swirling. Ginger's greeting had pushed his already unsteady feelings teetering on the cliff edge. Her embrace had been exactly what he needed. Someone to care. She'd made him realize there was a huge hole in his life he'd been ignoring for a long time.

He shouldn't take her attention personally. They barely knew each other. But she had a caring heart; she'd been alone and frightened. She would have welcomed Nels with the same enthusiasm.

He stepped into the master bedroom and paused. The room had never smelled like this before. A sweet, flowery scent hung in the air. He moved to the dresser near the bathroom door. The smell was stronger here. He forced his mind to focus on what he needed and not the heady scent of Ginger's fragrance. Pulling open the bottom drawer, he dug out sweatpants, a faded T-shirt and socks, then headed for the hall bathroom to change. The scent followed him.

By the time he returned to the living room, he'd managed to corral his scattered emotions, and shake off the chill around his heart and soul. Ginger was seated in front of the fireplace again and glanced over her shoulder as he approached.

"Feeling better?"

It was a simple question, but he had no simple answer. So he nodded and sat in the other chair where he'd been earlier.

"Sorry there's no coffee."

"How's Elliot? Was he scared?"

Ginger smiled. "He didn't budge. I checked on him several times, but I don't think he heard a thing."

He reached out and took her hand. "How about you? You going to be okay?"

She smiled, and his heart did a funny thump in his chest. Her pretty eyes filled with gratitude.

"I am now."

Ty chuckled, his gaze resting on Ginger's profile as she stared at the fire. There was something so comfortable about her, her greeting earlier opening a door to a part of him he'd kept sealed. A powerful need to confide overtook him. He'd never really been honest with the department shrink for fear his weaknesses might reflect badly on his record, hamper advancement and damage his reputation. Worse yet, if the other guys got wind of the humiliating details, he'd be an outcast, an object of scorn. The brotherhood was a complicated one. Often unfair and sometimes cruel.

Ginger tugged on her stray curl, running it through her fingers. No, confiding in her wasn't a good idea. She had enough burdens without him adding more. They held hands a long moment, then Ginger looked away toward the windows. "I think the storm has passed."

Ty released her hand and rose to go to the window as the power kicked back on. "Looks that way." He turned toward her. Her face was pulled into an adorable squint as she tried to adjust to the sudden light in the room. Her auburn hair shimmered with cinnamon highlights. She stood and walked to the kitchen island, and he allowed himself a quick flash of appreciation for her figure. Her waist was a perfect fit for a man's arms to hold. He looked away. "Well, I guess I'll head back to the boathouse." The TV flared to life again, and the weather map showed the storm had moved into the next county. Ty walked to the door, picking up his still-wet poncho. "I'll see you in the morning. Make extra coffee."

She nodded and smiled. "Maybe some biscuits to go with that?"

He winked. "That's what I'm talking about."

Chapter Six

Once the storm passed, Ginger slept soundly and woke refreshed and filled with hope. It had been a long time since she'd felt this way. The coffee was made and the biscuits in the oven when EJ padded into the kitchen. His eyes went immediately to Barney sitting on the counter.

"Mom, how did Barney get here? And why is the cereal all around him?"

"Beats me." She shrugged, playing along with the game Ty had started. "He was here when I got up, and I don't appreciate him eating after bedtime." She pointed at the dark crumbs. "He got into the cake, too. You really need to have a talk with him."

EJ stared at her a moment before a broad smile spread across his face. "Tyster told me to watch him. Guess I'll have to tie him down tonight."

"Good luck with that. I think he's a tricky one." Ginger ruffled her son's hair and pulled him into a hug about the time a short tap on the door sounded, and Ty walked in. He held his cell phone up, a huge smile on his face. "What's wrong?"

"Nothing. You won't believe the phone call I just got. Pastor Jim at our church has a job offer for you."

"What?"

Ty nodded, coming toward her, his smile broader than EJ's. "I mentioned to him yesterday at the service that you were looking for work, and gave him your qualifications. Well, it seems Babs Overby, the church secretary, is having surgery. She'll be out four to six weeks. They were going to hire a temp, but when I told Jim about you, he wanted to offer you the job."

Ginger stared at Ty, trying to grasp what he'd told her. "This is crazy. Things like this don't happen to me."

He chuckled. "How soon can you be ready? Jim wants to meet with you this morning."

"Uh, give me half an hour or so."

He laughed, waving his hand in the air. "Sorry. You don't really have to rush. Those biscuits smell great. We'll have breakfast, then I'll take you into town afterward."

"This is an answer to prayer."

He winked. "Yes. It is, isn't it?"

His comment struck a chord. She had prayed last night. For her mother, for herself and her future, but mostly for Ty's safe return. At this moment, all her prayers had been answered. Day by day she could feel the Lord calling her to Him, but why was God listening to her now, and not before, when she'd been so alone and desperate? The timer dinged on the oven, and she picked up the oven mitts, removed the sheet of biscuits from the rack and set it on the counter. Her thoughts cascaded erratically in her head. "Oh, what about EJ? I shouldn't take him on an interview."

"Don't worry about him. We'll hang out together." He poked the boy in the arm playfully.

Ginger raised her fingers to her lips. "And what about a car? How will I get to work?"

Ty took her hand. "I already thought of that. Matt has an old truck I can borrow. You can use my car until yours is fixed."

His thoughtfulness touched her. He'd stepped up and offered to solve her problems. What would it be like to have a man like this in her life—a partner, a friend, someone to share the joys and the struggles? "You've thought of everything."

"I try."

She pulled her gaze from his blue eyes as another obstacle presented itself. "I'll have to register Elliot for school if we're going to stay here awhile, but where should he go? What about after school? What are my hours? Who will watch him until I get home?" She sank onto one of the stools. "Ty, there's so much to work out."

"Don't worry." He laid his hand on hers. "I have a plan. We'll get you signed up for the job first. Then we'll register Elliot for school. After that, we'll go to lunch and work out the rest of the details."

Ty's reassuring words and kindness eased much of her concerns. "Thanks. How about a hot biscuit to celebrate?"

"Only if you have some grape jelly to go with them!"

Ty dribbled the basketball a couple times, then passed it off to Elliot. The church gym was empty, so he'd brought the boy here to shoot some hoops while they waited for Ginger. Elliot raised his arms and sent the ball into the air. It bounced off the rim and fell to the floor.

"Nice try. Next time, don't pull it back behind your head. Keep the ball in front of you and use your hands and fingers to direct it."

Elliot retrieved the ball and came to Ty's side. "Is my mom going to work here?"

"For a while."

"But it's a church, right?"

"Right."

"Mom and I never go to church. I think she's mad at God or something."

Ty exhaled a sigh. He'd suspected as much. If only he could make her understand that stepping away from the Lord was never the answer. Running toward Him, especially in difficult times, was best. "Well, maybe now she'll want to go."

Elliot thought that over as he bounced the ball a few times. "I hope so."

"I hope so, too."

A short while later, Ty heard the gym door open. Ginger came briskly toward them, the smile on her face bright enough to light the gym with its power. Ty tucked the ball under his arm and faced her. "Hey. Are you all set?"

She nodded, moving to her son and giving him a hug. "Are you having fun?"

"Tyster is showing me how to shoot hoops."

Her gaze locked on his. The happiness in her green eyes brought an extra glow to her pretty face. He wanted her to be this happy all the time.

"I'm hired. I start this afternoon. Mrs. Overby wants to go over my responsibilities."

"Then I guess we'd better get Elliot registered for school." Ty replaced the basketball in the gym storage room before heading toward the door. "I checked with my mother, and he'll go to the same school Kenny attends."

EJ smiled. "Really? I get to go to Kenny's school? Cool."

Ginger smoothed his hair. "I never thought I'd hear you so excited about school."

"That's 'cause I didn't have a friend before."

As they buckled into the car, Ginger exhaled a nervous breath. "I have so much to do. I need to dig out work clothes, do a load of laundry. Do you think I need to get a driver's license, or will mine be okay?"

Ty chuckled, reaching over to squeeze her hand. "You're good. Don't worry. We'll get it all handled."

Ginger smiled. "Thank you for being so helpful. I don't know how I would have managed without you."

"That's what I'm here for." He wondered if maybe there was more truth to that statement than he realized.

Ginger walked into her office at Peace Community the next morning, humming a cheery song she'd heard on the radio on the way to work. After a quick lunch yesterday she'd returned to the church office and spent the afternoon being trained by Mrs. Overby. Most of her responsibilities were simple, and she was familiar with the computer system they used. Ginger felt confident she could handle the job. She'd also been introduced to the staff and given a tour of the church.

Settling into her chair, she got to work, sending up a prayer of gratitude and marveling at the Lord's sense of humor. He'd answered her prayers by placing her in a church. A light tapping on the glass window separating her office from the hallway pulled her gaze away from the computer. Laura Durrant smiled at her.

"Good morning. Ty told us the good news about your job."

Ginger slid the glass panel aside, so they could talk. "I can't believe how quickly it all came together. And Elliot is thrilled about going to school with Kenny." Over the past two years her son had withdrawn into himself, and his grades had suffered, especially after they'd moved to the apartment. A few days in Dover, with fresh air, freedom to play and one-on-one attention from Ty, had brought about a dramatic change in Elliot. Herself, as well. The peaceful cabin and the new job gave her a sense of security and purpose, and a reason to hope again. "What are you doing here so early?"

Laura held up a folder. "I have some papers for Jim." She grinned and raised her eyebrows. "So, Ty has never brought anyone to meet the family before."

The implication sent heat rushing into Ginger's cheeks. "Oh, no. It's not like that. Ty's just helping us out."

"So it has nothing to do with him liking you?"

Ginger struggled to speak around the dryness in her throat. How was she supposed to respond to that? "No. We're just friends. We barely know each other."

Laura smiled. "If you say so. I'm in a hurry or we'd discuss this more. I want you to come to lunch at my house soon, so we can talk."

Ginger nodded. "I'd like that." She turned her attention to her work, puzzling over Laura's observation. Why would she think Ty was interested in her? She was positive Ty was simply being thoughtful, though she had to admit, the Sunday afternoon with the Durrants had been delightful, and being around Ty made her feel attractive and feminine.

Ginger had barely returned to her work when the pastor called her into his office, motioning her to be seated.

"How's it going so far?"

"Good. Everyone is very helpful, and I'm enjoying the work."

"Well, we'd like to make some changes in your responsibilities if you're willing."

A kernel of concern formed in her chest. Had she made a mistake already?

Jim leaned forward, resting his arms on the desk. "We have a family in our congregation who needs help. Their home was destroyed in a storm last month when a large tree fell on the house. The owner, Lee Stanton, was severely injured. He's a small business owner, and things have been tough for him lately. The church, in conjunction with the Handy Works ministry, are rebuilding their home."

"Handy Works?"

"It's a ministry started by some of our members. They do repairs, yard work and other small projects for the elderly and people unable to hire the work done. We've received a generous anonymous donation for materials for the Stantons' home, but what we really need are volunteers. We'd like to have the home ready for them to move back into as quickly as possible."

Ginger's heart was touched that the church would go to such lengths for one of its members. "What would you like me to do?"

"We need someone to recruit volunteers, schedule them to coincide with the various stages of the build, and also to line up volunteers to provide food each day." Jim smiled at her. "I know it's a lot to ask and a big change from what you thought you'd be doing, but it's important, and I think you would be perfect for the job."

The idea excited her. Organizing people was one of the things she enjoyed most. "I think it sounds challenging. I'd be happy to take that on. How soon do you need the volunteers to start?"

Jim tapped a folder on his desk. "Laura Durrant dropped these permits by this morning, so we can start construction immediately."

Ginger returned to her desk eager to start on her new assignment. It was a huge job, a lot of responsibility, but the challenge filled her with excitement. She was starting to believe her life was finally turning in a new direction.

April Craig walked into the office, peering over Ginger's shoulder. "I see you have our most-likely-to-volunteer list." The tall redhead was the music director for the church and backup secretary. Like Ginger, April was widowed. Their shared experience had bonded them quickly.

"I'm looking forward to this."

"Well, don't count on too many of them offering to help. I can tell you right now which ones will, and which ones won't."

Ginger glanced down at the sheet of names Jim had provided. "Why wouldn't they want to help?"

"Lots of reasons. Mainly they're too busy with their own lives. But this is the biggest project the church has ever taken on, and I don't have much hope of it getting done anytime soon."

Ginger refused to be discouraged. "Then it'll be my job to convince them it's a good cause."

"It *is* a good cause. A regular Dover do-over."

"What?"

April smiled. "Do Over. It's the original name of the town. A fire destroyed most of the town back in the early 1900s. When they rebuilt they decided to do a better job. A Do Over. Over the years the name got shortened to Dover."

Do Over. It's what Ginger needed. What she'd been

looking for. She never thought she'd find it in a small Mississippi town.

"Don't forget I'm taking you to lunch today."

"I'm looking forward to it."

"Me, too. Come by the choir room when you're ready, and we'll walk over to Magnolia Café."

Ty zipped his gym bag closed, flung it over his shoulder, then strode toward the door of the workout room at the Dover Police Department. Brady had invited him to use the equipment, and Ty had welcomed the opportunity. His five-mile run each morning had restored much of his stamina, but the strength training would get him back in top-notch shape to return to work. If that's what he decided to do.

"Glad to see you're taking me up on my offer."

Ty turned with a smile as he recognized Brady's voice. "I never pass up free, Chief. You should know that."

Brady chuckled. "Don't I know. Well, I have another freebie for you." He pulled a small card from his shirt pocket. "It's a guest pass for the firing range. I figured your shooting skills might be deteriorating."

A chill settled on Ty as he took the card. He glanced at his friend. Did Brady know about his dirty secret? Is that why he'd set this up? "Thanks."

Brady's eyebrows rose. "Sure. It's good through the end of the month. Just turn it in at the range when you leave town."

The chief studied him a moment, then tapped the guest card Ty still held. "Use that. You know how therapeutic firing a weapon can be. Releases all those pent-up emotions and clears the head."

"Right." Ty shoved the card into his back pocket and

gave his friend a quick salute. "I need to be going." Brady nodded, but Ty could feel his gaze boring into his back as he walked down the hall and out the door. Settled in his brother's truck, Ty gripped the steering wheel, attempting to control his anger. The firing range. The last place he wanted to go, and he was certain Brady knew the truth, or at least suspected it. Every time he thought about picking up his gun, he broke out in a cold sweat.

At the cabin, Ty parked and climbed out, dragging his gym bag with him. As he walked across the yard toward the boathouse, he glanced up the slope at the cabin. The *empty* cabin. This was crazy. Ginger had been on the job barely a full day, but he already missed her and EJ.

Inside the tiny boathouse, Ty stowed his gym bag, then slipped off his jacket. He'd come here to sort out his future, but all he'd been doing was thinking about a cinnamon-haired woman with deep green eyes and a little boy who brought a kind of joy into his life he didn't know he'd been missing.

Ty pulled the card Brady had given him from his back pocket and placed it on the small dining table, his gaze drifting to the closet where he kept his gun safe. He'd have to requalify with his firearm before he could return to duty. But it was a moot point if he couldn't get past the fear of picking it up.

He retrieved the small safe from the back of the closet, carried it to the kitchen table, put in the code and opened the top. The sight of the black steel SIG Sauer sent an electric jolt along his nerves. Gritting his teeth, he reached down. His hand started to shake. Icy fear exploded in his chest. Nausea pooled in his gut. He raked his hands through his hair. He wasn't afraid of anything, but he trembled like a scared kid when he tried to pick up his gun. It didn't make sense.

"Hey, Ty, you in there?"

The sound of his brother's voice yanked him from his thoughts. "Yeah, come on in." Matt joined him at the table, pointing to the gun safe.

"You have weapons here?"

Ty closed the lid and set the lock. "Just this one." He returned it to the closet and shut the door. "What brings you here in the middle of the day?"

His brother studied him a moment. "Are you okay? I won't pretend to understand what you're going through, but I can listen if you need to talk."

"I know. Thanks." He forced a smile, resting his hands on his hips. "I'll sort it out." Ty held his brother's gaze until he looked away. He did not want to talk about his fears at the moment.

Matt slipped his hands into his pockets and smiled. "Well, I promised to take Kenny to the Natural Science Museum and the Children's Museum in Jackson this Saturday, and I thought you and Elliot might want to tag along."

The idea chased away the last of his tension. Taking EJ on a day trip was a great idea. "Yeah, I think he'd like that."

"Do you think his mom will be okay with him going? She can tag along if she'd feel better. She doesn't know us very well."

Ty felt certain he could talk Ginger into the trip. "I'll work it out. Thanks. I think it'll be a fun day."

"Great. He slapped Ty on the shoulder with brotherly affection. "Hey, Dad told me he'd asked you to take on the foreman job for the Stanton house. You going to do it?"

"I don't know. I came here to think, not work."

"If you ask me, thinking is highly overrated. When I need to sort things out, it usually helps to keep my hands busy first."

"That's what Dad keeps telling me."

Matt chuckled. "I hate it when he's right."

After his brother left, Ty showered, then headed to the cabin for a bite to eat. He smiled when he saw the long row of small metal cars lined up on the kitchen island. EJ loved his little cars. The prospect of having a father-son day with the boy lightened his mood. Father-son? Where had that thought come from? He needed to nix that idea right now. This was not the time to be thinking about family.

Maybe taking on the house project was a good idea after all. The physical labor, other guys to hang with, would leave little time to think about his decision or his tenant. He wasn't getting anywhere sitting around here. Pulling out his phone, he called his dad and accepted the job.

Ginger checked another name off her list, then glanced at the clock. She was ten minutes late meeting April. Closing out her files, she picked up her purse and hurried down the hall. The choir room was empty. The lights were on, music flowed from somewhere, but no sign of April. Her gaze fell on the spinet piano set at an angle to the chairs arranged in rows on risers.

Since seeing the lovely baby grand at the Durrants' last Sunday, she'd been itching to play again. She had to do something while she waited. Sliding onto the piano bench, she flexed her fingers, then placed them on the keys, her mind pulling up a piece from her childhood. The ubiquitous "Für Elise."

Surprisingly, the notes flowed. Her fingers moved easily as if she'd never stopped playing. When she finished, she opened the sheet music on the stand and sight-read the notes.

"You never mentioned you could play." April leaned on the top of the piano, eyes wide.

"I've played most of my life up until about eight years ago. I miss it. I didn't realize how much until just now."

April frowned. "I'm sure there's a story there someplace. Why don't you tell me about it over lunch? Then I'll ask you to fill in on Wednesday nights for choir rehearsal since I just found out the regular pianist has decided to go back to school and get her degree."

"Are you serious?"

"That's why I was late. Oh, and the job pays money. Which I know is something you're fond of."

The idea intrigued her. "Would I have to play on Sundays, too?"

"No. Sarah Marsh will still play for the services, but she has a night class on Wednesday. By the way, we're adding a contemporary service in a few months, and I'm putting a praise band together. You could play the keyboard."

"Thanks, but I'm sure I'll be gone by then." Ginger stood and picked up her purse. "I'll have to find someone to watch Elliot on Wednesday nights."

"We'll work that out. There's always a solution, girlfriend."

Ginger was beginning to believe she was right. The extra money would not only help pay for the car, but she might be able to pay Ty back for all the things he'd provided.

Ginger took the stairs to the cabin deck with an extra bounce in her step that evening, eager to share her good news with Ty and EJ. Overseeing the volunteers for the Stantons' home build had fired her imagination, but playing the piano for the choir would add much-needed funds to her bank account. The thought of playing again filled her with a joy she'd long missed. Stepping from the chilly, dark evening into the warm, cozy cabin wrapped her in a blanket of security and contentment.

"Hey, Mom. We're making pizza. From patch."

Ty turned and smiled at her. "He means scratch."

Ginger placed her purse on the small table in the eating area and slipped off her coat. The sight of the two huddled over the counter made her smile. Ty included Elliot in everything, making him feel special and grown-up. The man had a warm heart and a generous spirit that was even more attractive than his handsome face. "Sounds like fun. Need any help?"

"The more, the merrier."

Ginger kicked off her shoes and hurried to the island, raising her eyebrows when she saw her son slicing an onion. "Where did you learn to do that?"

EJ grinned. "Tyster showed me how so I wouldn't cut my fingers off."

"I'm glad. Fingers come in handy from time to time."

Ty handed her a paring knife. "We have some peppers that need to be cleaned and diced."

"Yes, sir." After washing her hands, she joined them. The dough was already spread out on a large pizza pan, and Ty was opening a package of pepperoni. "I don't think I've ever had homemade pizza from patch before." She ruffled EJ's hair.

Ty huffed out a grunt. "Anyone can pick up a phone and order one. It takes great skill to create your own."

Ty walked to the fridge and pulled out several packages of cheese. She noticed his limp as he moved, triggering her concern. “Ty, are you all right? Did you hurt yourself?”

He kept his back to her, focusing on the packages in his hands. “No. I overdid it at the gym today, that’s all. I should have taken it slower.”

From the tone of his voice, it was clear he didn’t want to talk about it, so she let it drop for now. “Well, my day was very good. I took on another job. A paying one.”

“Yeah? Doing what?”

She couldn’t keep the smile from her face. “I’ll be playing the piano for choir practice on Wednesday nights.”

“That’s great.”

“It’ll be wonderful to play again. I didn’t realize how much I missed it until I saw the piano at your parents’. I’ll have to find someone to watch EJ those nights. Do you think your mom would let me leave him there?”

“Sure. She’d love it. But there’s no need. I’ll be here. I don’t mind watching him.”

“Oh, no, Ty. You’re doing so much already. I can’t ask anymore.”

“You’re not asking. I’m volunteering.” He turned to EJ. “What do you say, buddy? Can we spend a little more time together?”

EJ rolled his eyes, then stared at his mother. “Mom, me and Tyster are a team. Teams stick together.”

Ty stifled a smile. “He has a point.”

“Clearly I’m outnumbered.”

Ty and EJ exchanged smirks. “Yep.”

The pizza came out of the oven smelling delicious, making Ginger’s mouth water and her stomach rumble. “Should we invite Nels and Mae over to share this?”

"Oh, I meant to tell you. They left today to visit their daughter. They asked me to say goodbye to you, and they hope to see you again before you leave Dover."

"I hope so." She poured drinks and set them on the table while Ty sliced the pizza.

EJ slid into the chair at the small dining table and pulled a slice of pizza onto his plate. "Hey, Mom, can I have a bike? Please? There's plenty of room to ride around here, and I saw one on TV that was way super cool. It was black with fire decals and a red seat."

Ginger glanced at Ty, who shrugged and shook his head. "I don't know, sweetheart. We don't have room to take it with us, and I'm not sure if there'll be a place to ride at your grandmother's."

EJ slumped in his seat, the appeal of pizza gone. Ty and Ginger took their seats, and Ty offered up a blessing.

"I have something that might cheer you up, buddy." Ty laced his fingers and smiled. "You and I have been invited to go with Matt and Kenny up to Jackson this Saturday to visit the Natural Science and Children's museums."

EJ's eyes lit up. "Really? I always wanted to go to a museum. Can I go with them, Mom?"

Ginger's heart pinched with regret. There were so many experiences she'd wanted to give her son, but caring for John had taken all of her time and energy. It took her a moment to realize that Ty was speaking to her. "What?"

"I won't let him out of my sight. I promise, Ginger."

How could she refuse? "Of course he can go."

EJ hooted for joy, sharing a high five with Ty. Ginger looked on with a strange mixture of happiness and regret. Her son deserved a real family, a father who loved him and wanted to spend time with him. Ty was giving EJ a brief glimpse into what a father-son relationship could be. She prayed it would be enough to give him an understanding of what a man and a father should be. Ty was the perfect example.

"I have more good news to share."

Ty smiled over at her. "Oh, yeah?"

"I've been put in charge of the volunteers for a home the church is building for a family, and I'll be working with a ministry called—"

Ty paused with a hand full of pizza halfway to his mouth. "Handy Works."

"Yes. How did you know?"

He laid the pizza slice on the plate. "Handy Works is a ministry Laura and Matt started several years ago."

"I didn't know that. That's a wonderful service for the community." The look on his face pricked her curiosity. He seemed less than pleased.

"It is. And the Stanton project is important. Did Jim tell you what happened?"

She nodded. "I want to get as many people as possible lined up to work."

"Good. I'll need it."

"You?"

"I just took over as foreman for the job. You'll be checking in with me on the volunteers."

"Oh." She liked the idea of working with Ty, but he didn't seem too happy with the arrangement. Maybe he didn't want to spend any more time with her than necessary. Their lives had become very intertwined, and he'd come home for some solitude. Maybe he needed more space. "Well, I'm sure I can use your help."

"Laura usually oversees these big jobs, but with the

wedding coming up and restoring the house she and Adam will live in, she just doesn't have the time."

"So you're filling in?"

"No. I'm not a contractor, but her foreman, Shaw McKinney, is. He'll be in charge. My job is to make sure things are going smoothly on-site each day. The plan is to have this done by the end of the month."

Ginger stared at him. "Is that possible? To build a house in that short a time?"

Ty nodded. "With enough help and good coordination. But it'll be tough. This time of year, it gets dark at four in the afternoon, and January is our coldest and wettest month weather-wise. Fortunately, it's a small frame house on a conventional foundation, which makes things easier."

"You don't sound very confident."

Ty shook his head. "I just don't think we'll get enough people from the church to help. Not and have it done as quickly as Jim wants."

Ginger refused to be discouraged. "Then I'll just have to prove you wrong."

Ty gave her a skeptical smile. "I hope you do."

Chapter Seven

Ginger flipped on the blinker and made the turn from the county road onto a gravel driveway leading between giant oak trees. It had taken her a few minutes to figure out the GPS in Ty's car, but once she had, she'd found her way to the Stanton property easily. The trees opened up to a wide, grassy area filled with pickup trucks and cars parked around the foundation of the home where the exterior walls were being erected. Selecting an out-of-the-way spot, she parked and climbed out. Loud popping noises filled the air as another two-by-four section of wall was raised into place. She had no idea what was going on, but the thought of all these people here to help a family in need warmed her heart.

"Hello. I didn't expect to see you here."

Ginger glanced over at the woman approaching. It took her a moment to recognize Laura Durrant. "Hi. I could say the same." She looked completely different from last Sunday and even from yesterday morning. Stained and worn jeans were tucked into scuffed work boots. Her green T-shirt was faded and stretched out. A tool belt hung around her hips. Her hair, so long and lovely the other day, was caught up into a spiky knot on top of her head.

"My other jobs are on schedule, so I pulled some of my crew off to help over here. Shaw called in a few favors, too. Ty wants to get this roof done by the weekend."

"So fast?"

"I think so. With all of us, and the volunteers that you notified, and if the weather holds, we should be able to. So, what brings you to our job site?"

"I wanted a firsthand look. It's exciting seeing everyone come together like this to help a neighbor. Mainly I wanted to get a designated spot set up so everyone knows exactly where to put the food each day."

"I have the perfect spot."

Ginger followed Laura to an old garage located several yards back from the house. "We're using this space to store materials that need to be protected from weather. But I'll make sure we leave this side free for the food tables."

"Perfect. This way we can come and go, and not be in the way." Ginger watched the men working, her gaze scanning each pair of shoulders for one in particular.

"He's not here. Evans and Dabbs building supply donated felt paper and shingles for the roof. He's gone to McComb to pick it up."

Ginger blushed. "I wasn't… I mean, he's the only person I know who might be here."

"Oh, right." Laura winked at her.

"Well, I'd better get back to my car and watch for Sue and Doris Young. They're bringing lunch today."

"Before you go, can I ask you a question?"

"Yes, of course."

Laura pulled her aside, her expression clouded. "I'm worried about Ty. He's not his usual self."

Ginger frowned. "I'm not sure why you're asking me. I've only known him a short while."

"But you've been with him more than the family has. I can see he's troubled, but I don't know what to do. My parents are concerned, too."

She didn't want to betray Ty's confidence, but neither did she want his family to worry. "Ty has been through a life-changing event. That's not something you get over quickly."

Laura's blue eyes narrowed. "You sound like you're speaking from experience."

Ginger wasn't ready to get into her complicated past. "We all have situations in our life that are difficult to process."

Laura nodded thoughtfully. "I guess you're right. I was married before, and it ended badly. I had a lot of soul-searching to do before I could give my heart to Adam. It's just…Ty was so closed off last Sunday. He was scowling and grumpy all day. Usually he's the one joking around, but the only time he seemed like his old self was when he was talking to you or Elliot. You seem to have a connection with him we don't."

"Oh, I don't know about that." Ginger tugged on her hair, uncomfortable with the conversation. "Ty mentioned he'd come home for solitude so he could sort through the events surrounding his…injuries. Unfortunately, he came home to strangers in his cabin. I think he was expecting things here to be the same, but instead he came home to a new sister-in-law, a man he's never met is marrying his baby sister and taking over the family business, and his parents are thinking of retiring and moving away."

Moisture formed in Laura's blue eyes. "I never thought about it like that. But you're right. Ty got shot during the time Shelby and Matt were getting back together. Then Adam and I met, and got engaged on Thanksgiving Day."

"I think all he needs is time to work things out."

Laura rested her hands on her tool belt. "Ty's wanted to be a cop since he was five years old. Eventually, he'll go back to the force. You can bank on that."

Ginger's heart contracted. The thought of Ty picking up a gun and charging back into the world of big-city crime filled her with dread. What if the next time, the bullets claimed his life?

"As a kid, Ty was the champion of the smaller kids. He stood up to the bullies. I think he's only happy when he's helping people. It's who he is."

Laura's words settled like a stone in her heart. Was that why Ty had been so helpful? Because it was his nature? She'd hoped he was being kind because he liked them, her and Elliot. A flush of embarrassment stung her cheeks. She'd obviously read too much into Ty's attention. Silly her, thinking a man like Ty would be interested in a widow and her son.

"I hear Matt and Ty are going to Jackson on Saturday with the boys. Come to my house for lunch. I'll send you directions."

She probably should refuse, but she liked Laura, and having friends to talk to was something she'd sorely missed over the years. "I'd like that. Thank you."

Ty shut the door to the van and started around to the back, stopping abruptly when he smelled something delicious coming from nearby. He scanned the area, his gaze landing on the old garage where some of the workers had congregated. He smiled. The ladies of the church had come through again.

His sister met him as he approached the tables. "You just missed her."

"Who?"

"Ginger. She stopped by earlier to make arrangements for the food." She smiled and tilted her head. "She's really nice. I like her. We all do."

"Who all?"

"Mom. Dad. Matt. Shelby."

Ty knew the look in his sister's blue eyes. "You can stop the teasing. I'm just helping her out. Nothing more."

"Right. So you bring her to Sunday dinner."

"Trying to be neighborly." He started to move past her to the food table, but she caught his arm.

"Ty, I really do like her. She's sweet. I'm glad you were there to help her and Elliot."

"Me, too." Ty moved down the food table, loading up his plate with stick-to-your-ribs dishes that would fuel him for the rest of the day.

"This is quite a spread. Hope they feed us this way every day."

Ty glanced over his shoulder at the man behind him in line. At six-two and muscled like a navy SEAL, Shaw McKinney would have been an intimidating figure, except for his ready smile and quick wit. "I don't think you'll have to worry about the food with Ginger in charge."

"Ginger. Is that the very attractive lady staying with you?"

Ty frowned. "She's not *staying* with me. She and her son are in the cabin. I'm staying in the boathouse." Not that it was any of Shaw's concern. "What do you know about Ginger?"

Shaw picked up a plate. "Enough to know she's very

pretty, in a wholesome kind of way. She was here earlier. Hard to miss someone like her."

Ty set his jaw. He didn't like the idea of the men ogling Ginger. It would embarrass her. "Back off, Shaw. She's not your type."

"Oh, really? She might be the one to change my mind about settling down."

Ty doubted that. Shaw never dated a woman more than twice, and even that was rare. He wasn't a bad guy. He was a hard worker and dependable, but he liked to play up his reputation as a ladies' man. Still, he didn't want the man even *thinking* about Ginger. "She has a son."

Shaw growled. "Ah. That's a deal breaker. I don't do kids."

Ty smiled inwardly. Shaw might not, but Ty loved kids. EJ was proving to be his little buddy. After school they'd fish or play ball until it was dark. Someday, if things worked out, he'd like to have a whole house full of kids.

Daylight had nearly gone as Ginger began clearing her desk for the day. She'd lined up volunteers through the weekend, all with experience in rough carpentry and capable of getting the Stanton house under roof the way Ty wanted. But it had been a struggle. Finding people to provide food for the workers was an easier task. The ladies of Peace Community sought her out with offers. It was really very sweet and touching the way they all jumped in to do their part.

Tonight was her first time to play piano for choir rehearsal. And Ty had insisted on watching EJ after school. His reliability was admirable. It was nice to have someone to pitch in to help instead of having it all on her shoulders.

A light tapping on her door drew her attention.

"Mrs. Sloan? I'm Carol Stanton. Y'all are building our house."

A rush of joy and compassion surged through Ginger. She'd been looking forward to meeting the owners. "Mrs. Stanton, I'm so glad to meet you. I was going to come to see you at your place tomorrow."

A wan smile moved the woman's face. "We don't really have a place at the moment. Ben Campbell, the real estate man, he gave us a small house to stay in for now. I wanted to ask you to thank everyone for coming together to help us. My family is very grateful."

Ginger motioned for her to be seated. "It's our pleasure. Besides, I've learned a great deal about your family as I've talked to the church members. You and your husband are the first to step up when someone needs help. And I hear Mr. Stanton has coached various community teams for years. I think everyone is grateful for a chance to do something for you now."

Mrs. Stanton's eyes misted over. "I'm so thankful to the Lord for bringing such kind people into our lives." She stood, then said, "I have to get back to the hospital. I don't like to leave Lee alone too long."

"I'll keep in touch, and let you know how the house is progressing." Ginger spoke with the woman a few more minutes before saying goodbye. Having met Mrs. Stanton, Ginger was more determined than ever to find all the volunteers necessary to make this project a success.

Friday dawned cold and windy, and rain threatened. Ty stared up at the rafters being constructed above the Stantons' house. He'd wanted the roof finished by the weekend so they could start working inside, but they'd lost a whole day of work yesterday to rain, and several carpenters had left when they got paying jobs.

Shaw McKinney came toward him from the saw table where he'd been cutting lumber for the roof. "I take it Ginger hasn't been able to find any more willing workers?"

Ty shook his head. "She can find plenty of people to bring food, but not many who want to do the real work."

Shaw nodded. "Laura just texted me, she'll be pulling her guys off after today."

Ty exhaled a frustrated breath. Things were going much more slowly than he'd expected. "I had a trip planned with Matt and the boys tomorrow. Guess I should cancel."

"Nah. Don't do that. I'll be here all weekend. I've got a couple guys coming down from Jackson tomorrow to work. We should have it under roof by Monday. After that, though, I don't know what you're going to do."

"Pray." Getting this house done in a few weeks would need the whole town coming together. Ty was beginning to fear that might not happen.

The charming Victorian cottage in the middle of a tree-lined street elicited a sigh of appreciation from Ginger as she pulled into Laura's driveway Saturday. The house could have been lifted from a picture book. Intricate gingerbread dripped from every angle of the porch and gable. The broad wraparound front porch held planters filled with mums and colorful pansies.

She'd looked forward to lunch with Ty's sister, but a small part of her worried about getting too entangled with his family. Always in the back of her mind was the knowledge that she would be leaving as soon as she could pay for the car repairs. Her heart was tattered enough without ripping it more by leaving people she cared about behind.

Laura greeted her at the door with a bright smile and her little dog, Wally, who wagged his tail frantically at her arrival. Ginger rubbed his head, then followed Laura into the living room. The pleasing assortment of antique pieces, overstuffed furniture and cheery fabrics made her smile. “I love the way you’ve decorated, so cozy and comfortable. If I could design my dream home, it would look exactly like this.”

“Thank you. I’m going to miss it after Adam and I are married.”

“Ty mentioned you’re restoring an old home.”

Laura nodded. “I hate to sell, but we don’t need two homes. Come on into the sunroom. I have lunch all ready.”

The room captured Ginger’s heart. The large, glass-enclosed space was filled with light and inviting rattan furniture. A small table in the corner near the window faced out onto the winter garden where several large bushes were bent low with flowers. Pots of pansies brought color to the patio and the fountain, turned off for the season. “This is lovely. I’d spend every spare moment out here.”

“I try to, but the spare moments are becoming fewer and fewer.” Laura returned with two plates, drinks and fresh rolls on a large tray. “I’ve made you the only acceptable lunch for ladies of the south. Chicken salad, fruit, croissants and sweet tea.”

They chatted about the wedding and the work on the Stanton property as they ate. When Laura placed a slice of warm pecan pie in front of her, Ginger decided to seek the woman’s help. “I was wondering if there was a thrift store in town. Elliot has asked for a bike. His birthday is coming up, and I thought maybe I'd surprise him."

"There's a Salvation Army store just past the railroad tracks." Laura leaned forward. "When's his birthday?"

"A week from Sunday."

A huge smile lit Laura's face. "I have a great idea. Why don't we throw him a surprise party?"

"Oh, I'd love to do that, but I'm on a tight budget."

Laura waved off her concerns. "We'll keep it simple. A cake and gifts. We can have it at Mom's."

"Laura, that's too much."

"Nonsense. Mom and Shelby will be here shortly. We'll run the idea by them."

"Oh, then I'd better be going." Ginger started to rise, but Laura motioned her back down.

"We're going to be looking at wedding details, and I could use another woman's opinion. And I want you to come to the wedding. Please, say yes."

"But I'm not family, and I've only met your mother once and..."

"Once is enough. We all took to you right off. Besides, you're Ty's friend, so that means you're family."

Family. Ginger had never fully grasped the beauty of that word until now.

Stepping inside the beautiful sanctuary of Peace Community Church Sunday morning stirred up mixed emotions in Ginger's stomach. She'd been a freshman in college the last time she'd been in church. She'd decided to live her life on her own terms, unrestrained by her parents' dictates. Her nerves were on edge as she glanced around the sanctuary with its stained-glass windows, wooden pews and the large cross behind the pulpit. She wished she'd stayed at the cabin. She wasn't ready to face God yet. The touch of Ty's hand on her back stilled her troubled thoughts.

"Are you okay?"

She swallowed past the tightness in her throat. "It's been a long time."

His brows drew together in a frown. "But you work here now."

"Working in the office and worshipping in the sanctuary are two different things."

"I suppose so. But, you know, He's glad you're here."

Was God glad she was here? Or was He waiting to scold her for avoiding Him for all these years? She continued down the aisle, holding tightly to EJ's hand. Ty stopped at an empty pew near the front, waiting for her and EJ to sit. She was grateful for the separation her son provided. Ty had shown up at the cabin door in a suit and tie, looking as if he'd stepped off the cover of a men's fashion magazine. She found it hard to keep her eyes off him. And he smelled so good. Like soap and fresh air and pine. She really needed to get a grip on her growing attraction to him. Especially in church.

When the service started, Ginger braced for the old feelings of resentment to surface. Instead, she found a sense of calm settling on her shoulders. When they stood for the first hymn, Ty already had the hymnal open, holding it out for her to share. She grasped the edge, stealing a glance at him. His blue eyes were staring into hers, a warm smile lifting one corner of his mouth. When he started to sing in a rich baritone, she couldn't look away. It wasn't only that he knew the words, but he sang them with conviction. She wanted a faith like his. Solid. Strong.

Dependable. She'd had it once, but she didn't know how to get it back.

She turned her attention to Pastor Jim as he took the pulpit. After working with him all week, she was looking forward to hearing his sermon.

"Did God take something from you? Your spouse? Your health? Security?"

Ginger inhaled sharply. Was he talking to her?

"Are you angry with God because He didn't give you what you wanted or what you thought you deserved? Do you wonder why a loving God didn't make a world without pain and suffering, death and evil? What if I told you He did. But we thought we could do a better job of running the world. So we ate from the tree, and the world fell. God doesn't get back at us for what we do. But He did give us free will, and that means we must endure the consequences of our own actions and choices. It's easier to blame God. But when we do that, we don't mature. Trouble isn't to make us suffer, it's to make us grow and learn. So the next time we're faced with a difficult situation we'll apply the mistakes of the past and choose a better path."

The pastor's words landed like a pebble in her mind, stirring up a torrent of conflicting emotions. Wasn't that what she was trying to do—learn from her mistakes by staying out of debt and taking responsibility for her future? Hadn't she chosen a better path by reuniting with her mother and starting fresh?

Maybe she had drifted from her faith but she hadn't stopped believing. If God was so compassionate, why hadn't He intervened when she'd needed help? Why hadn't He answered her desperate prayers? Perhaps she was blaming God unfairly. If so, she had a long way to go before she could believe that He really loved her.

Ty took the last bite of his dessert, smiling as he watched EJ and Kenny enjoy the football game on TV with his dad. The boys were laughing and poking each other as if they'd been friends forever.

The trip to the museums yesterday had been a huge success. Both Kenny and EJ had delighted in every exhibit, dashing from one to the other, leaving him and Matt struggling to keep up. The day had given Ty a glimpse into his brother's life. Being a parent wasn't something Ty thought about, but today he'd thought of little else.

The only sour note in the trip had been the reports from Shaw. Ty had texted him several times for updates. The morning work had gone well, but midafternoon the rain had started and work had to be shut down. Structural inspections were due for Monday afternoon. They couldn't afford any delays, but that seemed to be the way things were going.

Carrying his empty plate to the kitchen, he realized Ginger was missing. She'd disappeared shortly after his family left. Matt had gone with Adam and Laura to their new home to discuss some construction details. Mom had joined Shelby and Cassidy to visit a friend who'd just had a baby. He hoped Ginger wasn't feeling left out, though he'd heard her decline when his mother invited her along.

He was curious to see how she'd liked his mom's famous Mississippi Mud Pie. If she was like most people, she'd fallen in love with the rich chocolate dessert after one bite.

Soft notes from the piano in the front room gave away Ginger's location. He strolled down the hallway, stopping at the archway into the living room, not wanting to disturb her as she played.

His gaze fell on her face with its creamy skin, long lashes and sweet mouth. That rebellious lock of hair dangled near her cheek, and he wished he could tug on it the way she always did. He leaned against the door frame watching, mesmerized by the serene expression on her face. She felt every note, her fingers and her heart intertwined. She ended the piece and rested her hands in her lap before glancing up and seeing him. A pretty blush touched her cheek. "Beautiful." The smile she gave him lit up her eyes.

"Thank you. I haven't played that piece in years. I'm surprised I could remember it."

Ty walked to the piano. "I wasn't talking about the music. I was talking about you. I've never seen you so happy."

She ducked her head. "I used to love to play. It was my escape. I could lose myself in the music and forget everything else."

"Then you should play as often as you can. You deserve to be happy." Something flitted through her eyes. Hope? Affection? Before he could name it she stood and glanced at the mantel clock.

"I think it's time to go. I need to get EJ ready for school."

"Sure." Ty followed her into the kitchen. She called to EJ, and both boys jumped up and dashed to her side.

"Do we have to leave? Kenny and I were going to play a game."

"Maybe next time. We need to get home…to the cabin, and get ready for tomorrow. Go find your jacket, and anything else you brought with you."

Ty stole a glance at Ginger. She'd called the cabin home. Did she think of it that way? He hoped so.

"I like your boy." Kenny tilted back his head and spoke bluntly to Ginger.

"Thank you, Kenny. And he likes you. I'm glad you two are friends."

The boy thought about that a moment, then nodded. "Me, too." He dashed off to sit with his grandpa on the sofa.

They made their goodbyes and headed to the car. Ty found himself smiling as he herded his guests to the vehicle. It was almost like having his own family.

Almost. But not really. The thought left a heavy sadness in his chest.

Falling asleep was impossible. Ty Durrant had taken up residence in her mind and refused to leave. He'd called her beautiful. The compliment had wrapped around her heart like a sweet embrace. She wanted to believe he meant it.

Closing her eyes, she willed herself to lock thoughts of Ty to the back of her mind. Tugging up the covers, she settled deeper into the bed. She'd been acutely aware of him all day. At his parents', he'd shed his suit coat and tie and rolled back the sleeves of his crisp, white shirt. He'd looked strong, handsome and compellingly male. It's one reason she'd retreated to the piano. Too much Ty Durrant wasn't good for a woman's heart.

Closing her eyes, she willed herself to sleep. When she woke again, the clock had barely moved. She started a mental list of all the reasons she shouldn't care for him, but found herself thinking of all the things she found appealing. Like his smile that weakened her knees. His caring heart. His respect for his family and others. His tenderness toward EJ. The way he made her feel special every moment.

She tossed off the covers and rose. At this rate she'd never get to sleep. Maybe a cup of hot chocolate would soothe her mind.

The sky was black as ink. If it weren't for the security floodlight shining through the trees from the far corner of the property Ty would have been in complete darkness. An owl hooted in the distance, adding an eerie tone to the dark night. He closed his eyes, only to open them again when he heard acorns crunching behind him and caught the scent of a flowery perfume on the air. Ginger. He should tell her to go away, to let him think. But he didn't want to.

She stopped beside the empty chair next to him. "Are you all right?"

The concern in her voice soothed his muddled thoughts. "As right as I can be." He risked looking at her, knowing his heart would stop briefly, then kick into high gear. Ginger made him think about his future, about a family. But the call to stay in law enforcement was too strong. It went deep into his heart and soul. His gaze slid to her face, shadowed except for the faint rays of the floodlight that kissed her cheek. Huddled inside her bright aqua sweater, her hands were buried deep in the baggy pockets. She was worried. He liked that she worried about him.

"I don't want to intrude, but I wanted to make sure you were okay. It's late and I was…worried."

He stretched out his hand. She hesitated a moment,

then clasped it. Her fingers were still warm. "Sit down. I could use a friend right now."

She settled into the other chair. He kept her hand in his, rubbing his thumb over the soft skin. "I should have listened to you the night of the storm and stayed at the cabin."

"Why? What happened?"

A short, bitter laugh escaped his throat. "I froze. Just like before."

Ginger leaned forward. "What do you mean?"

He struggled to find the right words. "I told you my partner died that day. But I didn't tell you it was my fault. We were making a routine follow-up on an investigation. A man appeared from nowhere with an assault rifle. I drew my weapon, but when I looked at the shooter, he was only a kid—no more than sixteen. I hesitated. Pete went down, and I took three rounds. Pete left a wife and child behind." He ran a hand down the side of his neck. "If I hadn't frozen, if I'd fired sooner, he'd be alive."

"You don't know that."

Her voice was soft and sympathetic. "Yes, I do. I screwed up when I should have acted. I don't think I can cut it anymore."

Ginger squeezed his fingers. "Have you talked to someone about this?"

"Sure. The department shrink. It's mandatory. He says until I deal with the real issue he won't sign off on my return to duty. He suggested I come home to think things through. I have to decide by the end of the month if I'm going back on duty or finding another line of work."

"What else would you do?"

He rubbed the side of his neck. "I have a masters in

criminal justice. There are a lot of private security firms that would hire me. Or I could go to law school."

"Those might be safer professions."

"Yeah, but that's just it." He turned to look at her. "I never thought about the risk before. I knew I could handle it. Now I feel…"

"Mortal?"

He nodded. It sounded lame when she said it out loud. He rested his head on the back of the chair, taking comfort from the touch of her hand. "I never wanted to be anything but a cop. I always knew it was what I was meant to be. No second thoughts. Ever. But now…"

"You have doubts."

"I question every thought. I'm like a truck stuck in the mud, just spinning my wheels and throwing dirt."

"We robbed you of your solitude. I'm sorry."

He looked into her eyes. They were filled with sadness, for him. Her mouth was pulled into a tiny frown that begged him to touch her lips. He squeezed her hand, so soft in his. "I'm glad you're here. You and EJ take my mind off my problems. And I needed to talk to someone. Thanks for listening."

Ginger shivered. He stood and pulled her up with him. "Come on. You need to go inside. It's too cold out here." He wrapped an arm around her shoulders, wanting to keep her warm, but as they walked toward the cabin, the closeness gave birth to other ideas. Ones he couldn't afford to explore. But she fit so perfectly against his side, and she smelled like flowers and night air. "I told you things I never told the shrink."

"Why didn't you tell him?"

"If certain things get into my files, it can affect future

promotions, and it doesn't sit well with the other guys if they know you're weak."

She stopped and laid her hand on his chest, forcing him to look at her. "You're not weak. You're one of the strongest men I've ever met."

He looked into her eyes, his heart swelling at the admiration displayed there. He shook his head. "You shame me, Ginger. You've carried a huge burden all alone, and still managed to remain kind and sweet, and raise a great kid in the process."

Her eyes widened, and her lips parted. He stared at her mouth, wondering what she tasted like. How she would feel in his arms. His hands gripped her shoulders, pulling her closer. He gazed into her eyes and found no resistance in the green depths. Slowly, he lowered his head, his lips touching hers for a brief moment. She swayed toward him before opening her eyes. He inhaled a shaky breath and forced himself to step back. "Go to bed. You're a working woman. You need your rest."

He watched her walk to the stairs and cross the deck before starting back to the boathouse. Something had shifted inside when he'd kissed her, leaving him confused and off balance. He had a feeling she'd felt it, too. One thing he knew for certain. One kiss from Ginger was not enough. It never would be.

The oven timer rang. Ginger inhaled the aroma of fresh blueberry muffins. Pulling the tin from the oven, she set them to cool while she finished getting ready for work. She'd offered to provide food for the workers at the Stanton house today.

"EJ. We're leaving for school in fifteen minutes." A muffled noise was the only response.

Glancing out the large front window, her gaze came to rest on the gnarled oak tree where she'd seen Ty last night. He'd looked so alone, huddled in the Adirondack chair. Her heart had gone out to him. She understood the mental struggles after a life crisis. All she'd intended to do was listen, but as he'd shared his fears, she'd found herself wanting to encourage him to walk away from police work. She'd started to care for him, and the thought of him charging into danger every day filled her with fear.

The kiss had further confused her thoughts. She'd replayed the moment dozens of times since last night. His strong hands on her shoulders pulling her toward him, the look of longing and curiosity in his blue eyes. She'd been unable to breathe anticipating his lips on hers. His kiss had been soft, tender, like a whisper of things to come. Ty Durrant was stirring feelings she'd never thought she'd experience again. Feelings she didn't know what to do with.

Chapter Eight

Ty climbed down the ladder and headed to the garage for a cup of coffee. He was tired, sore and hungry. Mainly he was reliving that kiss. He was supposed to be thinking about his decision, but all he could think about was kissing Ginger again.

He rubbed his forehead, inhaling the cool morning air and taking a quick glance at the Stanton house. The roof was on, ready for felt paper and shingles, and the exterior walls were being covered in insulation board. The weather had cooperated. Now the interior work could get underway, and they could work through the night, if necessary. Which was looking more and more like a distinct possibility.

"Good morning."

Ty turned around, nearly bumping into Ginger, who stood just outside the garage door. The sight of her made him smile. "Hello. I didn't expect to see you here." She smiled back, turning his insides to warm syrup.

"It's my day to bring breakfast." She held out a small tray with a variety of goodies. "I made the muffins and sausage balls. The homemade cinnamon rolls are Mrs. Ainsworth's."

Ty took a blueberry muffin from the tray, peeled back the paper and took a big bite. He'd had Ginger's muffins before, and he knew how delicious they were. "You should sell these."

"Do you think I could make enough to pay for my new transmission?"

"Definitely."

She glanced toward the house. "How's it going?

"The roof is on, but we can always use more volunteers. We need help installing the windows and putting on the siding. Even folks willing to clean up would save time."

"I never imagined it would be so difficult to find volunteers. I've already been through the members list. I talked to Jim about it, and he suggested I call Hope Chapel. Mr. Stanton's brother attends there, and they might be willing to help."

"Good idea. Be sure to remind them that we don't always need skilled people, just extra hands."

"That's good to know because many are worried they're not capable with tools." She smiled again and started to walk away.

"Where you going?"

"You're not the only hungry man on this job."

He watched her stroll toward the house, offering the tray of goodies to the crew. To a man, they all smiled when they looked at her.

After grabbing a large cup of coffee, Ty left the food table and headed across the yard. His gaze sought out Ginger, and he found her standing on the far side of the house talking to Shaw McKinney. Something in the way the carpenter was leaning toward her sent a finger of irritation down Ty's spine. Ginger was smiling.

Shaw laughed and bent toward her. Ty set his jaw. Ginger nodded, laughing out loud at something Shaw said. The sound of her laughter landed with a thud in his chest.

Ginger waved at Shaw, then walked back toward him. Ty's gaze darted between Shaw, who was watching her walk away, and Ginger, who had a silly smile on her face. She stopped in front of him and held out the tray. "There's one more blueberry muffin if you're interested."

"What did he say to you?"

"Who?"

"Shaw. Was he bothering you?"

"No. We were just talking."

Ty glanced over at the man who had his hands on his hips and an amused grin on his face. Shaw raised a two-finger salute. "You need to stay away from him. He's not the kind of guy you should encourage."

"Encourage?"

Ty sent a glare in Shaw's direction. "He's got a reputation."

"I'm sure he can't be that bad. I doubt your sister would hire someone who wasn't trustworthy. He was very nice. I liked him."

"He's not nice. He's…" Words failed him. How could he make her see that the man wasn't the type she should get involved with. "He's not the kind to commit."

"Who said I was looking for commitment?"

This wasn't going the way he intended. Ginger was glaring at him, her green eyes dark and stormy. Didn't she understand that he was just trying to protect her?

"I'm trying to tell you…"

"You're trying to tell me who I can and can't talk to?"

"No, I just don't want you to get hurt."

"Well, for your information, I liked Shaw. He was

sweet. You're my landlord, not my guardian. What I do and who I see are none of your business."

Ginger stomped off, leaving Ty standing alone and uncomfortably aware that his exchange with Ginger had called attention to himself. Landlord? Is that how she thought of him? After that kiss last night, he'd thought they were something more. Fine. If she wanted to get tangled up with a guy like Shaw, it was none of his concern.

Turning on his heel, Ty strode back to the house. He filled his apron with roofing nails, hoisted a fifty-pound bundle of shingles onto his shoulder and started up the ladder. On the roof, he dropped the bundle and glanced down to the yard. Ginger was climbing into her car. He exhaled a tense breath, then went to work.

Ginger dropped her purse on her desk and sat down, still mad at Ty's overbearing behavior. Did he think one kiss gave him the right to tell her what to do?

April looked up from the other desk, eyebrows raised to her hairline. "What happened to you?"

"Shaw McKinney."

A slow, dreamy smile softened April's features. "Yeah. He happens to all of us." She waved her hand in front of her face. "Gorgeous."

Ginger frowned. "I suppose, but that's not what I meant. I was talking to him at the site this morning, and Ty got all weird, talking about Shaw not being a nice guy, and that I should stay away from him." Ginger leaned back in her chair, arms over her chest. "Where does he get off telling me who I can talk to? Shaw was simply asking about the volunteers, and he complimented me on my muffins."

April laughed out loud. "Honey, don't you get it? Ty was jealous."

"What?"

"I've seen the way he looks at you, and I see your face when you talk about him. There's something going on between you two."

Ginger tried to hide the blush that burned her cheeks. "There's nothing going on."

"Uh-huh." April crossed her arms over her chest. "Has he kissed you yet?"

A small squeak escaped Ginger's mouth. "That is really none of your business."

"I knew it. Good for him." April leaned toward her, a smirk on her lips. "You can try and deny it, but I'm telling you, Ty was watching you smile at Shaw, and his blood started to boil. In his own twisted male way, he was trying to protect you."

Ginger thought that over. "He did say something about not wanting me to get hurt."

April nodded and pointed a finger at her. "If I was you, I'd be tickled to death that he was so upset. There's something real sweet about a man wanting to protect the woman he cares about."

Ginger mulled that over the rest of the day. Was that what he'd been doing? The idea sent a bubble of lightness in her chest. She'd tried to dismiss it as just a friendly peck, even though she'd sensed something more. If he was jealous, then that meant he had feelings for her. Maybe this attraction she'd felt between them was more personal than she'd thought.

Ty trudged across the deck that evening, bone-tired. A twinge of anxiety made him pause with his hand on the doorknob. He'd avoided Ginger this afternoon, leaving as soon as she'd arrived from work, to return to the job site and get a few more hours of work done.

But he couldn't avoid her indefinitely. Might as well face the music. No doubt Ginger would have a few more choice words for him about his behavior this morning. He couldn't blame her. He'd acted like an idiot. Opening the door, he stepped inside, a sharp pain in his left thigh wringing a soft gasp from his throat. So much for being in shape.

"Are you all right?"

He glanced over at Ginger, who stood near the sink. The concern in her gaze sent a warm sensation through his heart. "Yeah. I guess I overdid it today. I know one thing for sure. I don't want a career in construction."

"Tyster." EJ hurried forward and stopped in front of him, tilting his head back to smile up at him. "We're having tacos tonight."

"My favorite."

EJ frowned. "That's what you said about Mom's chicken, too."

"Well, that's because I like everything your mom makes." He smiled at Ginger, hoping to score a few points. She didn't smile back. Resigned, he started toward the sink to wash his hands, EJ sticking close at his side.

"It's all ready."

Ty took a seat at the small table in the eating area, stealing quick glances at Ginger, but he couldn't gauge her mood from her expression. Thankfully, EJ dominated the conversation for most of the meal. When the boy went to his room to play, Ty helped clean up, then sat back down at the table, releasing a groan as his sore muscles complained. He rubbed his shoulder, rotating it a few times to loosen up.

"Let me help."

Ginger's soft voice stilled him; her hands on his shoulders sent a rush of heat through his veins. Slowly, she began to massage his shoulders and neck. Her hands were strong and sure, finding the knots and working them loose. "You've done this before."

"I had to learn some techniques to help John."

Ty decided it was time to make things right. Reaching up, he took her wrists in his hands and gently pulled her arms down across his chest until her face was beside his. "I was a jerk this morning. Forgive me?"

"I'll think about it."

Ty closed his eyes as her breath caressed his cheek. "I was jealous."

"I figured that out."

He released her hands, turning to look at her. "Are you upset?" The smile she gave him sent his heart soaring. "I shouldn't have carried that bundle of shingles to the roof. I was trying to impress you, and you didn't even see me. Dumb, huh?"

"Yes." She crossed her arms over her chest, but there was a smile on her lips. "But I was impressed."

Happiness bubbled up inside his chest like a kid's first Christmas. Now he could sleep and dream of a green-eyed beauty who warmed his heart.

Ty inched his truck forward a few more feet. The line to pick up EJ from school was moving slowly today. He shifted in the seat, realizing that his shoulders didn't ache today, thanks to Ginger's skilled hands. Now if he could find more skilled hands to help at the Stantons', he'd be a lot more hopeful. He appreciated the members who had stepped up to volunteer. Each one had come with willing hands and loving hearts, reminding him how much Dover and its citizens meant to him. But they needed more help if they were going to have the job done on schedule.

Ty pulled the truck to a stop beside the school's side door, waiting as EJ climbed in, dumped his backpack on the floor and fastened his seat belt.

"How'd it go today, buddy?" Ty steered the vehicle to the end of the drive and around the cafeteria building, following the painted arrows on the asphalt to the exit. He looked forward to picking EJ up each day. They spent the afternoons together fishing, tossing a football or hiking the trails along the lake when the weather permitted. The boy was bright and curious, with a great sense of humor.

"Awesome. Tyster, do you like being a cop?"

Ty glanced over at him. The inquisitive brown eyes were watching him intently. "Yes. I do. Why do you ask?"

"Willy Sanders's dad came to the school today. He's a cop. I think cops are cool."

"You do?" A knot formed in Ty's chest. Ginger would not be pleased with his new interest. "Why's that?"

"They help people."

"They try. It's part of their job. Do you know what the policeman's motto is?" EJ shook his head. "To protect and serve."

"Is that why they have guns? To protect people?"

"Right."

"What's the serve part mean?"

"That's the helping part. Like after an accident or with an argument, things like that."

"The cops helped me and my mom after my dad got shot."

Ty inhaled slowly. This was a topic EJ should discuss with his mother. But he didn't want to discourage the boy from talking, either. "I'm glad to hear that."

"They came and talked to Mom, then they made us go stand with other people so we'd be safe. There were lots of policemen and firemen, and all kinds of trucks and stuff."

"That must have been scary."

EJ nodded. "My daddy took a ride in the ambulance."

"I know." EJ rode quietly for a while, and Ty assumed he was remembering the day his father was shot.

"Tyster? Do you have a gun and a badge?"

"Yes."

"Why don't you wear 'em? Cops wear guns. Willy's dad had a gun and a badge and handcuffs."

"I don't have my gun or badge right now because I'm on leave of absence."

"What's that mean?"

Unwilling to talk about the details of his shooting with the boy, Ty searched for a simple explanation. "I got injured on the job a few months ago, and I have to get better before I can go back to work."

EJ mulled that over a moment. "We all got to hold Willy's dad's badge. It was really heavy."

The simple statement landed like a stone in Ty's chest. The weight of that small badge had become heavier than he'd ever imagined.

He glanced at EJ, who was staring out the window. Should he encourage him to talk or let the subject rest? Maybe he should tell Ginger about the conversation. But then he'd be betraying EJ's trust. The boy was fishing for something. He just didn't know what. Maybe it was best he didn't interfere. If EJ brought up the subject again, then he'd mention it to Ginger.

Ginger pushed the start button on the dishwasher, then picked up the dishrag and wiped down the counter, draping it over the side of the sink when she finished. Cleanup had been quicker tonight. Ty had returned to the job site. She missed him. The cabin felt strange without his energetic presence.

She headed down the hall to her son's room. "Time to turn out the lights, sweetie."

EJ rolled onto his side, propping his head on his hand. "Mom, can we stay here?"

She sat down on the edge of the bed, reaching out to stroke his dark brown hair. "You mean in the cabin? We'll stay until we can go to Grandma's."

"No. I mean forever. I like it here."

A pit opened up in Ginger's stomach. "Elliot, this isn't our home. You know we're only here because of the car breaking down."

"I know, but I like my school, and I have friends, and everyone here is nice. Nobody yells or gets mad and stuff."

The pit in her stomach widened. The only memories her son had of his father was the shouting and anger. It wasn't a legacy she wanted him to have. "We've met a lot of nice people, but it's still not our home. We're just visiting—like a long vacation. You get to live in a cabin by the lake, go fishing, play ball with Ty and enjoy the Durrants on Sunday. That's a pretty cool vacation."

"That's why I want to stay. Ty and Kenny are my friends."

"And they are very good friends. We'll just have to

enjoy them as much as we can until we leave. You'll have lots of wonderful memories to take with you."

"You can't hug a memory."

Ginger pulled her son close. She was collecting a lot of memories herself. All of them involving Ty. Like remembering the feel of his strong arms, and the kiss that made her smile each time she thought about it. The cabin had become her fortress of safety and happiness, and Ty her knight in shining armor, standing guard to protect her. She wished she could stay here, too. But she wasn't a princess, and Ty wasn't a knight. He was a cop.

"Go to sleep, sweetheart. We'll talk more about this tomorrow."

Ty was tapping at the front door when she returned to the living room. He stepped inside, his expression revealing his fatigue. Her heart went out to him. He worked hard. She was certain he gave all his effort at whatever he tackled, whether building a house, enforcing the law or loving a family. Another reason to wish they could stay in Dover.

"Are you hungry?" He nodded, pulling off his coat and hanging it on the peg. "Go, sit down. I'll bring you a plate."

Ty took a seat on the sofa, one foot propped up on the coffee table, staring into the fireplace. She could tell by the slope of his shoulders he was worried about something. She handed him a plate of beef stew, then sat beside him, picking up one of the throw pillows and hugging it to her chest. She let him eat before she expressed her concern. "What's on your mind? The Stanton house or your future?"

He sighed, and shook his head. "I saw the volunteer list today. I know you're doing all you can, and I'm grateful for those who are willing to help, but we can't get this house done on time without more people."

Ginger's spirits sagged. Her efforts to recruit workers wasn't as fruitful as she'd hoped. She didn't like letting people down, especially Ty. "I'm so sorry. I was so sure I could convince everyone to help."

He squeezed her hand. "It's not your fault. Just the way it is."

"Can you hire the work done?"

"We could, but that would eat into the donation funds. We'd like to keep some in reserve to give the Stantons toward medical bills and living expenses after they come home."

Ginger understood the crushing burden of medical bills. "Do the volunteers have to come from churches?"

Ty looked up. "No. I guess not."

"Could they come from other organizations?"

"I suppose. Why?"

Ginger clasped his large hand in both of hers. "Well, I've been thinking."

He exhaled a huff of air. "Dad always groans when Mom says that."

"Hush. We found people at Hope Chapel willing to help. Maybe we should ask some of the other churches, and the police and fire departments. They might have people who would help."

Ty stared at her, his eyes warming with a smile. "You are a very smart lady. I should have thought of that. I'll talk to Brady first thing tomorrow. If we can get the windows in and the siding on in the next couple days, we'll be back on schedule." He reached out and tugged lightly on her stray curl. "Virginia Sloan, you are amazing."

Chapter Nine

The morning rain had moved out, leaving behind a clear, crisp and sunny afternoon. Perfect pigskin weather. Ty took several rapid steps backward, raising the football over his head and pointing with his free hand for EJ to go long. The boy backpedaled, raising his arms. Ty sent the ball through the chill air toward the boy, smiling as it landed in his arms, wobbled, then fell to the ground. He laughed. "Good try, buddy. You almost had it."

"You've lost your touch, Durrant."

Ty whirled around at the familiar voice. Brady Reynolds strolled slowly toward him across the yard. "Hey, what brings you out here? Don't you have important police work back in town?"

Brady extended his hand. "Nothing that can't wait." He smiled as EJ joined them. "You wouldn't know from that puny toss he just threw, but Ty used to be a pretty decent quarterback. 'Course, he was younger then."

EJ laughed and hugged the football. "Are you a policeman like Tyster?"

Brady raised an eyebrow at the nickname, slanting

a look at Ty. Ty shrugged. "Brady, this is Elliot Sloan. Ginger's son. EJ, this is my old friend Brady Reynolds."

"I'm the chief of police in Dover. That's better than being an ordinary detective." Brady leaned down and winked. "I get to drive a police car."

EJ's eyes widened. "Really? Did you bring it today?"

"Sure did. Want to go see it?"

EJ bounced with excitement. "Yes."

The trio walked around the cabin to the driveway where the black-and-white cruiser was parked.

"So, what are you really doing here, Brady?"

"Just on a call, and thought I'd swing by and see how the Stanton project is coming along. I'm scheduled to work this Saturday along with several of my guys."

"That's great. We might get this house back on schedule after all." Ty stopped beside the cruiser parked behind his truck.

"Wow." EJ stared in awe at the vehicle. "Can I sit inside?"

Brady chuckled and unlocked the car. "Sure. I'll show you where all the cool gadgets are."

EJ slid in behind the wheel while Brady hunkered down and pointed out all the equipment, from dashboard computer and sirens to lights and scanners.

Ty crossed his arms over his chest, smiling at the boy's delight. EJ was a great kid. He'd miss him when he left. A lump formed suddenly in his chest. He'd miss him a lot.

The SUV pulling into the drive diverted his attention. Ginger was home, and he hadn't even thought about supper. But inventing new meals was something they both enjoyed. He watched her climb from the car, but the expression on her face put a knot in his gut. Her green eyes were dark with fury. Her mouth set in a hard, angry line.

She strode to the patrol car, searing him with a scalding glare before turning her burning gaze on her son. “Elliot. Get out of there and go inside. Right now.”

Brady rose and stepped back, a deep frown on his face, his hand holding the car door open.

“But, Mom, Brady was showing me all the cool stuff in the police car. I even got to…”

“Now! Go!”

EJ started to speak, but Ginger jabbed her finger toward the house. He obeyed without a word, but the tears in his eyes revealed his hurt feelings. Ginger turned and glared at Ty. He suddenly felt like a kid who’d ruined his mother’s prize china figurine. He fell back on habit. “Uh, Brady, this is Ginger Sloan, EJ’s mother. Ginger, this is Chief Brady Reynolds.”

“Ma’am.” Brady touched his hat, then sent a sympathetic glance at Ty before sliding behind the wheel and starting the engine. “We’ll talk later.”

Ty watched the car pull away and drive off, dreading what was to come. Steeling himself, he faced Ginger. And knew he was about to get reamed.

It was all Ginger could do to hold her tongue as she stormed around the cabin and out onto the pier. She needed time to get her anger under control before talking to EJ. The sound of boots on the wooden planks alerted her to Ty’s presence. She turned and unleashed her anger. “What are you doing letting my son play in a police car?”

“He wasn’t playing. He was exploring. Brady was showing him the equipment, that’s all.”

“*That’s all?* Are you serious? I have enough trouble keeping his hero worship for you under control. He thinks you're some kind of superhero. I took some comfort from the fact that you aren't really a policeman here. No gun. No badge. Just a guy. But now, you're feeding his fantasies by showing him all the nifty gadgets you danger junkies play with."

"Ginger..."

She held up her hand to stop him. "But you never tell him about the ugly part. The risk, the pain. How could you do that when you know how I feel about your job, and guns, and all that comes with them? I don't want him dreaming about being a cop."

Ty frowned, placing his hands on his hips. "He's almost eight. He'll want to be a dozen different things by the time he has to decide."

Ginger shook her head. "No. Ty, this isn't going to work. I appreciate all you've done for us. Especially with Elliot, but I think it would be best if you backed off on your relationship with my son. It's going to be hard enough for him when we leave. We might as well start putting some distance between us before we get entangled in each other's lives more than we already are."

"Ginger, I think you're overreacting."

"Am I? He's a very impressionable little boy. He told me about the policeman who visited the school yesterday, and now he's sitting in a real police car. I don't want his head filled with dreams that could get him hurt."

"I would never hurt him. You know that."

"Not on purpose, but you are. You're glorifying a profession I don't want him thinking about. It's got to stop. Now."

She watched as his blue eyes darkened, then narrowed. His jaw tightened, the muscle flexing rapidly. "Fine. You want distance. You got it."

He strode briskly toward the boathouse. Ginger held her breath, anger and fear pulsing in her veins. She'd hurt him, but she'd had no choice. He didn't understand the way a little boy thought. Ty was a grown man. In time he'd come to see she was right. The argument only pointed up how comfortable she'd gotten here and how dependent she was on Ty's help. But it wasn't too late. All she had to do was focus on her job, get the stupid car paid for and get to Arizona.

Inhaling a ragged breath, she started back to the cabin. Now she had EJ to deal with. How could she make him understand? The aftermath of her anger left her shaky and drained. As she crossed the deck, she saw the lights go out in the boathouse and Ty emerge. He had his duffel in his hand and his computer case over his shoulder. He crossed the lawn with long, determined strides, disappearing around the side of the cabin. The sound of the truck door slamming and the motor roaring to life signaled his departure.

Ty was leaving. She felt cold all over. It was best this way. Time apart would give them all a chance to regain perspective. But as she stood on the deck, a powerful and unexpected wave of loneliness rushed through her, bringing tears to her eyes. How would she get along without Ty? She closed her eyes and dug deep. She didn't need Ty Durrant. She'd come this far on her own; she'd go the rest of the way. She'd been distracted by the safety and comfort of Dover, of the Durrants. Her long-held dream of love and family had materialized, and she'd allowed herself to indulge in the fantasy.

She opened the cabin door. Fantasy time was over. Seeing EJ in the police car, and the uniformed officer with a gun on his hip, had hit her like a sledgehammer in the chest. She saw clearly what Ty did for a living, and the repercussions of that profession. She'd been living in denial about his job. Cooking together, working on the project, losing her heart to him, had made it easy to forget what he was.

Inside, she glanced around for her son, but the living room was empty. He was probably in his room. As she walked down the hall, she tried to find a simple way to explain her anger over seeing him in a police car. How could she make him understand that she didn't want him dreaming of being a policeman? It was dangerous. He could get hurt or worse. Injured like his father.

EJ was stretched out on the bed when she peeked in. Barney Brim in his hands. His sweet face was pulled into a dejected frown. Steeling herself, she sat on the edge of the bed. His dark brown eyes, so like his father's, looked up full of questions and confusion.

"What did I do wrong, Mom?"

She reached out and stroked his silky dark hair. "Nothing, honey. I shouldn't have shouted at you."

"I was just looking at the police car. I didn't break anything. Honest."

"I know. But when I saw you in that car…it made me think of how dangerous a policeman's job is."

"But policemen help people, too. They're heroes."

"You're right."

EJ sat up. "So can I go talk to Ty?"

"Ty's decided to stay at his parents' house for a while. They miss him."

Elliot sat up, his mouth in a tight line. "No, he didn't. You made him go, didn't you? You don't like him."

"That's not true."

"Yes, it is. I love Ty, and you're mean." He ran out of the room.

She heard the door slam as he went outside, and the sound of his pounding feet on the deck as he went. Ginger raked her fingers through her hair. What a mess she'd made. She was only now beginning to realize the consequences of her outburst. Who would pick EJ up from school tomorrow and watch him? Would Ty ask them to leave the cabin now? Would he want his car back? Hers still wasn't ready.

Maybe she should apologize and ask him to come back. No, that would be grossly unfair. Using his kindness to get herself out of a difficult situation was out of the question. He deserved better. He'd been a kind and generous friend. She exhaled a sigh. She'd deal with Ty tomorrow. First, she had to make things right with her son. But how?

Ty opened the back door to his parents' home, his heart heavy, his guilt even heavier. What had he been thinking? He should have anticipated Ginger's reaction to finding EJ in the cruiser. He knew what she feared most.

His mother was curled up in the family room with a book and glanced up as he entered, her expression revealing her surprise. She'd probably been expecting his dad. "Hey, Mom."

"Ty, sweetheart. What brings you by today?" She laid her book down and came to him, hands touching his cheeks lovingly. "I'm so glad to see you. But something is wrong. I can see it in your eyes. Do you want something to eat or drink?"

He shook his head, setting his duffel on the floor. His mother noticed it and frowned.

"Ty? What's going on?"

"I thought I'd come home for a couple of days, if that's all right."

"Of course it is, but you've been pretty firm about not staying here." She took his arm and steered him toward the kitchen. "Sit."

He did as he was told, knowing what was coming next. A glass of cold milk and a plate of chocolate chip cookies. Apparently, no matter how old a guy got, or how dangerous his job, his mom thought cookies and milk were the way to open him up.

He rested his elbows on the granite kitchen counter until his mom had poured herself a cup of hot tea and set the snack in front of him. "I feel like I'm ten years old again."

"You look like it, too. Now, what's going on?"

"I screwed up, Mom. With Ginger. Big-time."

"I'm sorry to hear that. I like her. I think you two might have a real connection."

"Meaning?" He took a cookie from the plate.

"That you're attracted to each other. You seem comfortable together. It's nice. And that little boy adores you."

"He's a great kid. But as for me and Ginger, that's not going to happen. I've told you before, women don't want to get involved with cops. It's rough, never knowing if your husband will come home, waiting for the phone call and the officers to show up at your front door."

"Has she said that?"

He nodded. "Loud and clear."

"I'm surprised. She seems like such a strong young woman."

"She is. Strongest woman I ever met. Even more than Laura, and she's pretty tough." He laughed softly.

"Does she have a reason to feel this way about your job?"

"A good one. Her husband was a security guard. He was shot and left paralyzed. He died last year from his injuries, but the shooting has left Ginger with a deep fear of guns and violence, and life in general, I think. Getting involved with a cop isn't something she's looking to do."

"I see. So, how did you mess up?"

Ty clasped his hands together in front of him on the counter. "Brady Reynolds stopped by the cabin in his patrol car. EJ was with me, and he was all excited about the car. So Brady let him sit behind the wheel and toy with some of the equipment. He was having so much fun, it never occurred to me to tone it down."

"Then Ginger came home and found her son captivated by a police car?"

"How did you guess?"

"I'm a mother. I could see where this was going."

"Wish I would have. Ginger was furious. She chewed me out big-time and..." He glanced away toward the back window, trying to ease the sting of her words. "She asked me to back off from EJ. She doesn't want us spending so much time together." His mother reached over and rested her hand on his forearm.

"I'm so sorry, son. Maybe after she has time to cool down, she'll change her mind. I don't imagine EJ is going to be too happy about you leaving."

"No. We've become close. I look forward to our afternoons together."

"Well, you can stay here as long as you like. You know that."

"Thanks, Mom." The rattle of the back door sounded as Tom Durrant walked into the room.

"Hey, Tyler. Or should I say *Tyster?*" He came over and patted his shoulder. "You come to have supper with the old folks?"

"Supper. Breakfast. Whatever else."

"Oh? What's going on?"

Ty made a hasty explanation, omitting some of what he'd told his mother.

"You know what? This is actually perfect timing. I've got a Handy Works project that I've been needing to do, but most guys I know are tied up with the Stanton house. I think you and I can get it done in a day if you're up to it."

Ty eyed his dad suspiciously. It wouldn't be the first time he'd been drawn into a project that was more work than he'd expected. "Go on."

"There's this elderly couple out on Holt Road, Jean and Ross Carter, who have an old shed that needs to be torn down and hauled off. They found a vagrant sleeping in there a few weeks ago. Scared them pretty bad. What do you say? Provided you can get away from the project house."

Ty nodded. "Shaw McKinney is taking over for the weekend. Who's going to watch the store?"

"Adam's got it under control. That boy's a born merchant."

Ty wasn't in the mood to hear the praises of his oh-so-perfect, soon-to-be brother-in-law. "Sure. Fine. When do you want to start?"

Dad smiled. "The crack of early tomorrow. It's been a long time since we've had any father-son time. This'll be great. I'll schedule a Dumpster to be delivered out there first thing tomorrow. I hear Ginger has tapped into a new source of volunteers?"

"Yeah, she's called a couple other churches, and we've contacted the Dover police and fire. Several of those guys have construction experience. The plumbing crew should finish up today, and electrical said they'd wrap up tomorrow. That puts us back on schedule."

"Good to hear. Lee Stanton is a good man." His dad held his gaze a moment, a faint smile brightening his eyes. "Ginger's a very strong young woman. One of a kind."

"Yes. She is."

"As long as you're aware of that fact."

Later, as he settled into his old room, thoughts of Ginger filled his mind. She never ceased to amaze him with her strength and determination. But he didn't like her and EJ being out at the cabin alone. Nels and Mae were out of town. There would be no one around to help if they needed it. And who would pick EJ up after school?

Remorse blanketed his mind. He should have thought it through before letting EJ inspect the cruiser. He knew how Ginger felt, but at the time all he could think of was giving him a fun experience.

On the other hand, this separation was her idea. She was strong and capable. She'd lived her whole life without his help, and she'd managed just fine. The distance would do him good. He'd gotten far too involved in their lives. He had major issues of his own to work through. But he couldn't shake the feeling that taking care of Ginger and EJ was his job.

"You ready?" Ty watched the side-view mirror of the truck for his father's signal. When his dad dropped his hand, Ty let off the brake, easing the truck forward. The heavy-gauge chain they'd attached to the hitch bucked as it tightened. They'd spent the morning stabilizing the old shed on the Carters' property by tying it off to the surrounding trees. They'd dismantled the roof and taken down the rafters. All that remained was to pull down the four walls. Strategically placed ropes would insure the frame fell toward the center of the slab.

Ty pressed firmly on the gas, one eye on his father's image in the mirror directing him. The chain groaned. His dad took several steps backward. A loud crack rent the air, followed by a splintering sound as the four walls collapsed. Ty braked, turned off the engine, then hopped out, joining his dad at the pile of rubble. "That went well."

His father chuckled, pulling his gloves from his back pocket. "Now the dirty work begins."

Ty rubbed the side of his neck. "Yeah. Cleanup was never my thing."

"No kidding. Most of your mother's gray hair is from trying to get you to pick up your messes. Grab the chain saw. I'm ready to get this done."

An hour later, Ty removed his gloves and moved to the ice chest in the bed of his dad's pickup, pulling out a bottle of water. His gaze traveled back to the old shed, now a pile of rubble in the field beside the Carter house. The physical exertion had drained off much of his inner frustration and cleared his head.

His dad hoisted himself up onto the tailgate. "We should be able to finish this up in another hour or so. The truck is coming to haul off the Dumpster at three."

"Good. Can we eat lunch first?"

"Might as well."

Inside the cab, Ty took a bite of the turkey sandwich

his mom had prepared for them. Sensing his father's gaze, he glanced over at him. "What?"

His father studied him a moment. "Don't you think it's time to get things off your chest?"

"What are you talking about?"

His dad snorted softly. "You may be a grown man, son, but I'm still your father, and I know when you're troubled." He took a swig of his water. "It's not easy coming back from a traumatic event. It changes you. Messes with your head and fills you with doubts."

Ty didn't want to have this conversation. His mother always gave him space and time to work through his issues in his own way. His dad wanted to push and prod, and get to the heart of the matter. "You wouldn't understand."

"I understand completely. I've been where you are, Ty, and it's terrifying."

Ty shook his head. "Dad, no one knows what I'm dealing with. How could you?"

His father's eyes darkened, and his jaw set in a hard line. "I know because I had a close call with death, too. That auto accident I was in when you were a kid nearly shattered our family."

Ty remembered it well. He just hadn't made the connection to his own situation. Maybe his dad did understand. "How did you get through it?"

"First, I had to get past the silly fear."

"What?"

"That senseless fear that blocks you from moving forward. It's usually something that has no connection to your trauma. For me it was a fear of putting gas in my car."

Ty huffed out a sour laugh. "That doesn't make sense."

"It does when you look closer. In my mind, if I didn't put gas in the car, I couldn't drive. If I couldn't drive, then I couldn't have another accident."

Ty stared out the window. It was a twisted kind of logic, but in a way it did make sense.

"So, what's your silly fear?"

He rubbed his fingers over the scar on his neck. Admitting his fear, even to his dad, wasn't easy, but he wasn't getting anywhere on his own. "I can't pick up my firearm. Each time I try, I get the shakes. Brady gave me a pass to the firing range, but I can't bring myself to go." He raked his hand through his hair. "I can't be a cop if I can't handle a gun."

"I don't think your fear has anything to do with the gun. Think about it. If you don't pick up your weapon, you can't make any more mistakes. No one can get hurt."

He wanted to believe his father had a valid point. But it couldn't be that simple. "So, is that it? You just got over the fear?"

"Hardly. It also took a lot of prayer, support from your mom and determination."

His dad reached over and patted his knee. "Look, sooner or later we all have to face our own mortality. Even Lazarus died eventually. Once I accepted that, things started to improve. I decided to lean on the Lord more, trust Him more."

"But how? How do you let go?"

"It's a choice. Choose to stay in the pit of fear and guilt, or choose to let go and move forward. You've chosen a risky profession, but it's one I truly believe the Lord has called you to. But you've got to face the fear first, or you'll be stuck in that hole forever."

Ty mulled over his father's advice the rest of the night, but kept coming back to the same sticking point. Telling someone to get over it might be good advice, but how did you choose to face a fear that had a boot heel on your throat?

His dad had mentioned determination. Maybe that was the key. If he was determined enough, then he might be able to push past the fear. The first chance he got, he'd go to the firing range and test out just how determined he really was to remain a cop.

At least it was a start.

Chapter Ten

No way was this carton going to get the best of her.

Ginger huffed out an exasperated breath, sending the strand of hair on her cheek lifting upward briefly. She'd picked up Elliot's bike, and an employee had loaded it into the back of Ty's SUV, but when she'd arrived at the cabin she'd realized getting it out of the car and up the steps to the deck was another matter. It wasn't heavy, simply awkward. Three attempts at dragging it up the stairs had left her frustrated and admitting defeat. She needed help. Ty's help. Which meant she'd have to swallow her pride, again, and call him.

EJ was spending the morning with Kenny. She'd wanted to get the bike put together and hidden before he came home, but she had to face the fact that even if she managed to get the box upstairs, she had no idea how to put the thing together. She'd been so anxious to save money by foregoing the setup fee, she'd failed to think things through.

Pulling out her phone, she selected Ty's number, hesitating before placing the call. She missed him. Nothing was the same without him. She missed the sound of his laughter, the way he'd smile and wink when he was teasing her. She missed his strong male presence and the scent of earth and soap when he entered the room. She missed standing beside him preparing meals at the end of the day.

Maybe she'd been too hard on him about the police car. Once they left Dover and reached her mother's, Elliot would probably find new things to excite him. With a sigh, she pushed Ty's number on her phone and waited.

"Hello?"

The sound of his voice on the other end sent a wave of comfort through her. "Hi."

"Ginger? Is everything okay?"

She smiled. How typical of him to think of her first. "Yes. Fine. But I do need your help with something."

"Name it."

"I bought Elliot a bike. The one he's been wanting."

"That's great. He'll be pumped."

She sighed. "Not unless he can actually ride it. I have to put it together, and I don't have a clue where to start." His amused laughter filled her ear, bringing a smile to her lips.

"I'll be right over. Hey, where's EJ?"

"He spent the night with your nephew. He and Kenny have big plans for today."

"No doubt. I hope Kenny doesn't spill the beans about the surprise party tomorrow."

"Shelby assured me she had it handled."

"Good. I'll be home, uh, there, quick as I can."

Ginger ended the call, holding the phone against her chest. Ty was coming home. Her heart raced with anticipation. She'd missed him. Had he missed them, too?

* * *

Ty parked the truck near the cabin and climbed out, his gaze landing on the large box leaning against the steps. He smiled. He could imagine Ginger wrestling it out of his SUV and trying to drag it up the stairs.

He grabbed the hand holes and carried the carton up to the deck, leaning it against the rail before moving to the front door. He tapped his knuckles lightly on the glass pane. The thought of seeing Ginger again sent his heart racing. The fact that she'd called him and asked for his help gave him hope that she was no longer angry.

The door opened, and he gazed into her green eyes. He wanted to believe what he saw reflected there. She was glad to see him. He cleared his throat. "Good morning. I'm here to assemble a bike."

She motioned him inside. "Thanks so much, Ty. I really appreciate this."

"Glad I could help." The sight of her warmed him clear through. She was dressed in her favorite faded jeans, the ones that made her legs look a mile long, and a dark green shirt that matched her eyes.

"I should have paid the extra fee for assembly, but I'd already spent too much on the bike." She shrugged and smiled.

"Hey, no big deal. I used to put bikes together at Dad's store. I'm a certified professional."

"Oh. I didn't know your dad sold bikes. Maybe I should have purchased it from him?"

"No. He quit carrying them after the toy store opened." Ty retrieved his toolbox from the closet beside the laundry and carried it outside. Ginger shrugged on her bright aqua sweater and followed him, curling up in the rocker. "Can I help?"

"Sure. Somebody has to read the instructions and hand me the tools."

"I thought you knew how to do this."

"I do. But just in case bikes have changed since I did the last one."

She smiled at his teasing, and his heart pumped out an extra beat inside his chest. Lifting a box cutter from the top tray of his toolbox, he slit the carton open, keeping one side intact to use the cardboard as a base from which to assemble the bike and not lose any important parts.

Ginger sighed, watching him intently. "I never would have been able to put this together."

Ty sat back on his heels, hands resting on his thighs. "Sure you could. Just might have taken you a little longer."

"Like until EJ's next birthday." She smiled and hugged her sweater closer. "It's cold out here. You sure you don't want to do this inside?"

"I'm good." He unwrapped the bike seat and set it aside, then opened the box of parts and spread them out. He worked silently for a long while. Ginger seemed content to watch, and he was content to let her.

The bike was coming together quickly. He stood and tilted it onto its back wheel, giving the front one a quick inspection, then checked the rear wheel. Satisfied, he laid the bike down and tackled the kickstand. The comfortable silence gave him the courage to speak. "Ginger, I want to apologize for the other day."

She went still. Maybe this wasn't the right time after all, but it had to be addressed. "I should have thought about how EJ would react to the police car. It just didn't occur to me."

Ginger shifted her position, placing both feet on the

deck, leaning forward to look at him. "No, I'm sorry, Ty. I overreacted. Seeing that police car at the cabin, hearing Elliot's excitement over it, scared me. I don't want my son to grow up to be a police officer."

Her words stung. But he swallowed the hurt. He was aware of the stigma, but it had never been so personal before.

"What you do is an honorable profession. But the danger, the uncertainty, I could never live with that."

Ty tightened down the nut holding the kickstand in place with more force than necessary. He'd heard this lament more times than he cared to remember. His job was too dangerous. Too uncertain. He agreed, but this time the statement tore a hole in his heart.

"I should never have lashed out at you that way. It was a knee-jerk reaction. Will you forgive me?"

Ty looked into her eyes and had the oddest feeling he'd forgive this woman anything. "Already done. And I promise not to glamorize police work to EJ. I'll keep my job out of our conversations as much as possible."

"Thank you."

Ty gave the bike another once-over, then lowered the kickstand and stood back. "Mission accomplished."

Ginger stood and reached out to touch the silver-and-black bicycle with its red racing stripes and shiny pedals. "He's going to be so surprised. I probably shouldn't have spent the money, but he's been so good. He hasn't had a nice birthday since he was five. Thank you."

"It still needs the decals put on, but I'll do that later. I'll take this over to my parents. Dad can hide it in the garage until the party tomorrow. I'll put this in the truck and then come back and clean up."

After securing the bike, Ty returned to the deck, gathering up the scraps and folding the cardboard. Ginger had gone inside. He tapped on the door before entering. The cabin was warm and cozy, and the aroma of fresh coffee welcomed him back. He belonged here. So did she. Ginger handed him a cup, stepping aside to let him doctor it to taste. Now was the perfect time to make his suggestion. "Have you and EJ been okay here—alone, I mean?"

She hesitated a moment before answering "We have. Though the floodlight went out. It was really dark at night. It would have been nice to have you here."

The look in her eyes encouraged him. "I think I'd better move back into the boathouse. I don't feel right leaving you two out here alone. It's too isolated." He tried to gauge her reaction. "If it's all right with you, that is."

She sighed. "I'd like that. I like to think I'm brave and strong and all that, but truth is, I was scared out here alone. I feel safer with you here."

His heart pounded in his rib cage. He reached out and took her shoulders in his hands, looked at her lips. He wanted to kiss her again, but now might not be the best time. Instead he placed a kiss on her forehead. "I've missed you. I'll bring my stuff over later this afternoon."

"Oh. Okay."

The disappointment in her voice made him think she wanted him to come back immediately. "I'd get my stuff right now, but—" he rubbed his neck, dreading what he had to tell her "—the Stanton house was vandalized last night." Her soft gasp and the shock and tears in her eyes tore through his heart. "That's where I was when you called."

"Oh, no. Why would someone do that?"

"I don't know. Brady has his men looking into it. Shaw discovered it this morning."

"How bad?"

Ty exhaled a slow sigh. "Bad. They broke all the windows and tore off part of the siding. They trashed the stack of drywall stored inside and pulled out most of the electrical wiring. Most of the tiles for the flooring were smashed. Not one box left intact."

"What does this mean for the project? Can it still be done on time?"

"Doubtful. This'll set the completion back a couple of weeks." Which meant neither he nor Ginger would be there when the project was completed, something he had hoped to avoid.

"Oh, no, Ty, it can't. Mrs. Stanton is counting on bringing her husband home to their house. She told me yesterday that the place Ben Campbell loaned them has been sold. They won't have anywhere else to go but to a hotel. We can't let that happen. What are we going to do?"

"We're assessing the damage, then we'll have to see if there's enough of the donated funds to replace everything. But there's no way we can replace the time it'll take to redo the work."

"Has anyone told the Stantons?"

"No. We want to have a plan in place first. We're hoping we'll only lose a few weeks. It's not ideal, but at least the house will be done. I've got to go." He pulled her into his arms for a quick hug. "Don't worry. It'll all work out. I need to get back to the site. I'll be back as soon as I can."

She smiled and nodded, her eyes brightening. "Okay. I'll be here."

He liked the thought of her being there, waiting for

him to come home. As he drove off, a warm contentment washed over him. He was a man with purpose.

Butterflies waged aerial warfare in Ginger's stomach as Ty drove them to his parents' after church. She prayed the day would go smoothly, and this would be the best birthday of EJ's life. She was so grateful to the Durrants for putting the celebration together. She couldn't wait to see EJ's expression when he saw the new bike. He would be so surprised.

They'd had a small celebration this morning. Ty had made pancakes, Barney had been decorated with streamers, and balloons had guarded the small assortment of presents. If her son had been disappointed by not getting a bike, he hadn't shown it. He'd thanked her for the gift card and given Ty a big hug for the youth football and the Dover cap.

She had decided to give Elliot the bike last. Otherwise he would never open his other presents. Ty pulled the car to a stop in front of the Durrants' home. He gave her a wink before getting out. EJ ran ahead onto the porch, football under his arm, baseball cap on his head. Ty opened the door, shouting out a greeting as they entered the foyer. "Hey. Anybody here?"

They walked through the front room toward the kitchen. Ty took her hand and squeezed it. Ginger's heart fluttered. She was falling in love with Ty. She knew it wasn't wise, but her heart had other ideas.

EJ stepped into the kitchen, and everyone yelled, "Happy birthday!"

A huge smile spread across his face. He turned to look at her. "Is this my birthday party?"

Ginger hugged him. "It's all for you. Happy birthday."

Kenny rushed forward, smiling. "We surprised you, didn't we?"

EJ nodded. Kenny tugged on Elliot's sleeve. "Come on. There's lots of presents."

The Durrants greeted her with smiles and laughter, commenting on Elliot's response as they drifted into the family room, where the presents were arranged on the coffee table. Elliot stared at the gifts, obviously trying to decide which one to open first.

Kenny solved the problem by picking up a large package wrapped in bright red paper. "Open this one first. It's from us."

EJ tore into the paper, releasing a loud yelp as he unwrapped a bright blue remote-control car. "Mom. Look. Isn't it awesome? I always wanted one of these."

Kenny bounced on his feet. "I brought mine so we can race 'em."

"Cool." The next package, a handheld electronic game player from Laura and Adam, elicited another squeal of delight. "This is so cool. I always wanted an EGP."

Ginger's heart lodged in her throat. If she'd been able to envision the perfect birthday for her son, it would have been exactly like this. Ty leaned close, sending awareness along her nerves. "I think he's having a great birthday. Just wait till he sees the bike."

Ginger pressed her palms together, resting the tips of her fingers against her lips. Her heart was so full, she wasn't sure she could handle any more happiness. Closing her eyes briefly, she thanked the Lord for this blessing and for bringing her to Dover, to the doorstep of the Durrants. When she opened her eyes again, Elliot had opened a gift card from Mr. and Mrs. Durrant to buy games and movies for his player. The last gift was from

Ty. Surprised, she looked up at him. "You already got him a gift."

He shrugged and flashed his smile. "A kid can never have too many birthday presents."

EJ let out a shout when the paper fell away to reveal a shiny new fishing pole. He turned and smiled at Ty. "It's just like yours."

Ty nodded and gave a thumbs-up.

Ginger's gaze traveled around the room, taking a mental picture of the moment. Tom and Angie Durrant were standing in front of the fireplace, smiles brightening their faces as they watched EJ enjoy his party. Matt and Shelby were seated on the sofa, her hand resting on his knee possessively. Cassidy sat on her knees in front of them as they watched the activity. Laura and her fiancé, Adam, were seated in the two occasional chairs but had their hands linked across the small table dividing them. It was a portrait of family togetherness.

Ty rested his hand on her back, jolting her out of her reverie and making her aware of the tangy scent she'd come to know as his own. She wanted to lean against him, to feel the solid strength of him against her back, like a safety barrier. But she couldn't.

Elliot appeared in front of her, remote-control car in hand. "Can I take this outside and play with it?"

She smiled. "Did you thank everyone for their presents?"

He turned and glanced around the room. "Thank you. I love all my presents."

Angie Durrant came and gave him a quick hug. "You're most welcome, Elliot. And we have a cake for you, too." She pointed to the breakfast table, where a sheet cake decorated with cars rested.

Elliot smiled ear to ear. "Thank you."

EJ and Kenny disappeared out the door to play with their cars while the adults regrouped in the kitchen. The men decided to oversee the car race with the boys, while the women cleaned up. Ginger started to help, but Angie shooed her away.

"Go and watch your son play. Let us know when you're ready to bring out his bike."

"I can't wait to see that," Laura chimed in.

Shelby, hands full of discarded wrapping paper, joined them. "He is the cutest little guy. The look on his face was priceless. Matt took pictures. I'll get them to you later."

Out on the back porch, Ginger stood at the rail watching the boys guide the small cars along the driveway, noting with a smile that the big boys were itching to get their hands on the controls. After a few minutes, Ty joined her.

"Are you ready for the last gift?"

"I think so."

Ty took her hand, and they made their way toward the garage. The family had all agreed to park on the street so the driveway would be clear for the bike. Ginger waited near the garage door as Ty went inside and pressed the opener. The boys were so occupied with their cars, they didn't even notice the door going up.

Ty rolled the bike out of the garage. "Hey, EJ. You have one more present. Come and see."

Ginger took a deep breath, her gaze focused on Elliot. He'd stopped a few feet away. His eyes growing wide, his mouth open in surprise. She thought she saw a hint of tears in his brown eyes. Her heart overflowed with happiness.

"Oh, wow! Wow!" He jumped up and down, making fists of triumph in the air. "Thank you, Mom. Thank you, thank you." He gave her a big hug before approaching the bike. He touched the seat and the wheels before lifting the helmet from the handlebars. “Awesome.”

“Now you have to learn to ride it.”

“I kinda know. I’ve tried Kenny’s a couple times.”

The men gathered around her son. Tom Durrant ruffled his hair. “Let’s see how she handles.”

Adam and Matt exclaimed over the design, and Ty helped him adjust the strap on the helmet so it fit properly. Sensing her presence was no longer needed, Ginger retreated to the back porch to watch, trying not to worry about possible injuries.

Watching the Durrants as they helped her son learn to ride his new bike was like seeing her deepest dream come to life. This was what she wanted for her son. A family.

Emotions swelled in her chest. Tears filled her eyes. Unwilling to break down in front of everyone, she went inside, hurrying through the house and out onto the front porch. At the railing she stopped, letting the joyful tears overflow. Why couldn’t she have this all the time? Love. Family. A safe place to stay.

“Ginger?”

The sound of Ty’s voice penetrated her tears. She froze, unwilling to let him see her like this. Quickly, she swiped at her damp cheeks, digging in the pocket of her slacks for a tissue and coming up empty. A clean one appeared in front of her, held out by Ty’s strong hand. “Thank you.”

“Are you all right?”

She shook her head, then shrugged. “I guess. Maybe.” The confusion in her mind triggered more tears. What a silly mess she was. Her emotions were spilling out like a leaky dam. Happiness and frustration warred with gratitude and sorrow.

"What's wrong? Did something happen? Did someone say something that upset you?"

Gentle hands turned her around. She looked up into his concerned blue eyes and felt her emotional dam burst. "No, it's me. I'm so happy and grateful, but I'm angry and..." The tears poured out anew.

Ty pulled her into his arms, holding her securely against his chest, his hand cradling her head. She cried, knowing she was soaking his shirt with her tears, but unable to stop. Being in his embrace was so comforting, so safe. She wanted to stay there forever, knowing he would always protect her, watch over her.

The thought brought a cold rush of realization. She pulled out of his embrace, but he held on to her shoulders.

"Feeling better?"

"I..." She looked into his eyes and forgot to breathe. She needed to move away, put some distance between them, but she didn't want to. She wanted to stay right where she was, in his arms.

He reached out and laid his hand on the side of her face, his thumb gently stroking her cheek. "You're not used to all this happiness, are you?"

She tried to speak, but her throat was too tight. She shook her head.

Ty bent his head and looked into her eyes. "I'd like to see you happy all the time, Ginger. You deserve that and much more."

She looked down, her gaze falling in the center of his chest. "That's sweet, but no one is happy all the time. It's been an emotional day, that's all. Seeing EJ so happy is a dream come true. I wish..."

"Wish what?" He eased her closer, her hands pressing against his heart. It was beating as fast as hers.

"Nothing."

"Tell me your wish, Ginger, and I'll see if I can make it come true."

Before she could speak, he captured her mouth, stealing all the strength from her knees. She melted against him, her arms sliding around his neck. His lips were gentle, and, oh, so tender. He pulled her closer, deepening the kiss. Her knees threatened to give way as her insides melted. She lost all sense of time and place. There was only him. She wanted to stay in this moment forever.

He ended the kiss. Her mind floated a moment before settling back into reality. She looked into his blue eyes and saw confusion.

"Ginger, I..."

Was he already regretting kissing her? She stepped back, out of his reach, and hurried into the house, swiping away fresh tears. She knew the truth now, but it only served to complicate her already crazy life. Ducking into the living room, she took a couple deep breaths to calm her nerves. What did she do now? That heart-stopping kiss had exposed the truth. She'd fallen in love with Ty Durrant.

Chapter Eleven

"Mom, can I play basketball? The school is starting a team."

Ginger filled the plate with a small helping of chicken and noodles, then set it before her son. "EJ, we'll be leaving in a couple of weeks. You know that."

"Aw." He rested his head on his hand, poking at his food. Ginger filled her own plate, echoing a mental moan of her own. Her heart had started to grow roots in Dover, and to the man who'd taken over her every thought.

She glanced up as Ty walked in. Her cheeks warmed as her mind replayed yesterday's kiss. He'd been quiet on the way home from his parents' and had retreated to the boathouse when they'd arrived. Just as well. After that kiss, she had a lot to think about. He probably did, too. "Are you hungry?"

"I'll pick something up on the way. Brady wants me to guard the Stantons' house tonight. He's shorthanded."

Since the vandalism last Friday night, the Dover police had increased patrols, and the church had hired off-duty officers to stand guard; but the thought of Ty being out there terrified her. "Alone?"

He came and stood in front of her, a knowing grin on his handsome face. He reached out and touched her hair. "I'll be fine. I doubt if they'll come back. They know we're watching the place. It's just a precaution."

"Be careful. I couldn't stand it if…"

He hushed her, pulling her close against him. "Don't think that way. I'll be home before you know it."

"I feel so helpless. I wish there was something I could do."

"Keep digging up volunteers. That's what we need the most."

An idea formed in Ginger's mind. "Ty, how many people has the Handy Works ministry helped?"

He shrugged. "I don't know. Hundreds, I guess. Why?"

She wasn't ready to share her idea. It was still percolating in her mind. "Nothing. I just wondered."

"I've got to run."

She watched him go, stopping to speak to EJ before he headed out the door. Her appetite gone, she entertained EJ by making brownies and watching a movie. But the minutes crawled by. Her thoughts were consumed with worry about all that could go wrong. What if it wasn't just a few men, but a gang? What if they returned with guns, and Ty was unarmed? What if they snuck up on him and… She groaned. It was all too horrible to think about.

How did the spouses of policemen do it? She could never live with the constant worry, never knowing if he would come home again. John's shooting had been random. Wrong place, wrong time. But Ty put his life on the line every day by choice. How could she open herself up to that kind of danger? How could she ask EJ to possibly lose another father?

Worn down from worry, she prepared for bed, then

slipped under the covers, praying for Ty's safety. She tried to think about how capable he was, how strong. He was a trained officer with years of experience. John had been a security guard only a few months and viewed it as a game. But, despite Ty's skill and ability, he still had been shot.

She needed to stop this and focus on something positive. The vandalism had left a deep wound in her heart. There had to be some way to let people know of the need for volunteers, the importance of finishing the house. If only there was a way to reach all of the citizens of Dover at one time. A new idea bloomed. Maybe there was.

Her eyelids grew heavy, only to open again as she heard Ty's truck pull in below nearby.

He was home. Safe.

She closed her eyes and drifted off to sleep.

Ty slowed his truck, waiting for the car ahead of him to make the turn into the Stantons' driveway the next afternoon. He'd spent the morning going over the financial details with the anonymous donor's attorney. There was enough money to replace all the materials and hire the labor, but that would drain the funds and leave the Stantons with crushing medical bills. Something he was unwilling to accept.

As he drove into the large yard, he bent his head to peer out of the windshield. The Stantons' yard was a beehive of activity. Twice the normal number of vehicles were parked on the grounds. A delivery truck was offloading a stack of drywall. Men were unloading boxes of tile and buckets of thin set from a van. Electrical and plumbing trucks were parked near the side of the house.

His sister met him as he got out of the truck. "Can you believe this?"

"What's going on? Where did all these people come from?"

Laura looked at him with a puzzled expression. "Didn't you hear her on the radio this morning?"

"I was at Mac Bridges's office going over the finances. Hear who?"

"Ty, this is all because of Ginger. She is amazing. She went on WDVZ this morning and told everyone about the Stantons. She talked about how the church is rebuilding the Stantons' home, and the anonymous donor, and about being vandalized. And then—" Laura poked him in the chest for emphasis "—she mentioned Handy Works and called upon anyone who'd been helped by the ministry to show their gratitude by lending a hand on the Stanton project."

"Ginger did that?"

Laura smiled and nodded. "She also asked for donations, so that the Stantons could come home to a finished house and not be saddled with huge hospital bills."

Ty tried to process what Laura was telling him. "So all these people are here to help?"

"Yes, and I'm getting calls from local businesses wanting to make donations. The siding is going to be completely replaced at no cost, including labor. The electrical and plumbing are already here and working for free."

"How did she get on the radio? She never said a word about this."

"I don't know. But it's an answer to a prayer." Laura caught his gaze, her blue eyes narrowed and intense. "Tyler Wallace Durrant. She is one special woman, and if you don't claim her, you'll be making a huge mistake."

His sister was right. His heart was so full of love and pride for Ginger's ingenuity and hard work, he wanted to shout out loud. His gaze scanned the large number of volunteers. Thanks to Ginger, the house would be finished on time. None of this would have been possible without her caring heart. She'd found a way to make it all work, to overcome all the obstacles. If he hadn't already lost his heart to her, he definitely would have after this.

Maybe it was time to give up law enforcement. Having a woman like Ginger at his side, sharing his life, would be a blessing. As soon as he had a free moment, he'd do a little research and see what his options were. But first, he had to show her how much she'd touched him.

Today would go down as one of her all-time favorites. Ginger gazed across her desk to the rainbow bouquet of roses sitting before her. Ty had sent her flowers. She couldn't wipe the smile from her face. She'd asked the deliveryman twice who they were for. The last time she'd received flowers she'd been twelve, and her father had presented her with a small bouquet after one of her piano recitals.

Lifting the small card from the plastic holder she read the words again. "'To my Super Hero. You're amazing. Ty.'" Like the other dozen times she'd read the card, her heart fluttered.

When she'd called to thank him, he'd told her it was his way of letting her know how much the radio interview had meant to him, and how proud he was of her. She couldn't wait to see him tonight and thank him in person. Every gesture he made, every kind thought, just made it harder for her to leave Dover. But the time was coming.

Her gaze landed on the roses again, and she shoved

the future aside. She wasn't going to spoil this moment with thoughts of tomorrow. Ty had sent her flowers, and that's all she wanted to think about now.

The rain had started midafternoon, so Ty had left the site a little early. With all the extra help, he'd felt confident leaving the volunteers in Shaw's capable hands. He'd retrieved his laptop from the boathouse and made a dash through the rain to the cabin. The moment he stepped over the threshold, a sense of home enveloped him. The feeling went far beyond owning the property. The cabin held a welcoming comfort now, something that had been missing until Ginger and EJ had entered his life.

Which was why he was willing to think about a different direction for his life. He'd be a fool if he didn't at least consider a new future. One that included her and EJ.

Opening his laptop, he turned his attention to the screen. A few taps on the keyboard pulled up information on jobs for people with a law enforcement background. Maybe security work was the answer; keep the badge and the weapon, but lose the dangerous side of police work.

The list of openings showed promise, with salaries triple what he made now. With a sigh, he leaned back in the kitchen stool, absently rubbing the side of his neck. He felt certain he could land a position quickly. He had the credentials and the experience. But the motivation was lacking.

What about law school? He surfed online until a list of local colleges appeared. A small knot formed in his chest at the thought of going back to school, buried in law books. Neither option sparked a fire in his belly. The only fire in him right now was the lingering memory of Ginger in his arms, holding her close, and kissing her.

If he left the police, he might have a future with Ginger and EJ. But what kind of husband and father would he be if he gave up his calling? Would his dissatisfaction eat away at the relationship? She deserved all of him, not a watered-down version.

He shut the laptop and stood. Closing his eyes, he offered up another heartfelt prayer. *Lord, I need answers. I need direction. You're my strong tower. I need Your strength to fight the fear and doubt. Show me what I need to do to overcome my confusion.*

Ginger's hopes of spending time with Ty that evening were pushed aside. Her success at recruiting volunteers and donations had resulted in him spending more hours at the job site in order to get the house done on time. He'd left the moment she'd arrived home, but not before taking a moment to caress her cheek lovingly and dazzle her with one of his smiles.

After putting EJ to bed, Ginger headed to the living room, looking for something to occupy her mind. She spied Ty's laptop on the coffee table.

Opening it, the screen displayed the website of a local law school. Was Ty considering getting a degree? Did this mean he had decided to leave the police force? Her heartbeat quickened. No more danger. No more worry. She knew they had feelings for one another. The kiss proved that. She could so easily see a future for them. EJ adored him. But not as long as he was a cop. But as a lawyer…

She closed the computer, trying not to read too much into what she'd found. She wanted to talk to him about his decision, encourage him to leave the force. But he had to make his own decision. She needed to give him space and time to decide. Still, she couldn't stop the bubble of hope that floated to the surface of her mind.

* * *

Ty stared at the bobber as it floated on the water. He had no concern for the fish that might snag his line; his thoughts were focused on the boy beside him, sitting hunched over his new fishing pole, his forehead creased in a deep frown. EJ had been unusually quiet since Ty had picked him up from school.

The weather had turned warm and sunny today, and after completing his homework, EJ had asked to go fishing. They'd been sitting on the pier for a while now.

"Tyster, did you get shot?"

The question pierced right to his heart. He inhaled slowly, gauging his response. "Who told you about that?"

"Kenny. He said you were in the hospital a long time."

Ty looked at the bobber again, wishing he could float on the top of this issue and not get pulled under the surface. "Yes, I did." He waited for another question, but the boy fell silent again.

"My dad got shot. He couldn't walk anymore."

A lump formed in Ty's throat. Poor kid. "Yeah. Your mom told me." EJ turned and looked up at him, brown eyes moist with unshed tears. His bottom lip quivered.

"It was my fault."

"No, EJ. It wasn't your fault. It was the bad guy's fault."

EJ shook his head, one small hand still holding tightly to the pole like a lifeline. "I made him go back inside to get me a better toy. I already had the one in the box."

Ty searched for a way to handle this conversation. EJ should be talking to his mother, but he'd chosen to share it with him. "EJ, sometimes bad things happen to people, and when it does, we need a reason to help us understand. Sometimes we blame ourselves."

"But my dad said he would be okay if we'd never gone to that place."

Laying aside his pole, Ty wrapped an arm around EJ's slender shoulders and pulled him close. "Your dad was probably scared about not being able to walk again, and it made him angry. He worried about how he would take care of you and your mom."

"But what if it *was* my fault?"

"It wasn't. Believe me. Have you talked to your mom about this?"

He shook his head. "She might not love me anymore."

"Oh, EJ. Your mom will always love you. Nothing you could ever do or say will change that."

"But what if it was?"

Ty exhaled a long sigh. "I know how it feels to think that. When I got shot, my partner got shot, too. He died. I feel like it was my fault because I didn't react fast enough."

"Was it your fault?"

The question hit its mark. He thought about Julie, Pete's wife. She'd told him repeatedly it wasn't his fault, that she didn't blame him. "I don't know, buddy. I'm still trying to sort that out."

"Mrs. Graves in Sunday school told us when we have problems we're supposed to give them to Jesus because He's stronger than we are."

"That's true."

EJ's big brown eyes were filled with sadness as he looked up at him. "I don't know how to do that."

Ty cradled the boy's head against his shoulder. "I don't either, EJ."

"Maybe we should pray. Isn't that the only way to talk to Jesus?"

Oh, the simple faith of a child. "That's a good idea." Ty gently took the boy's free hand in his. "How about this? We each put our guilty feelings in our hand. Then we'll pray and give them to God. When we're done, we'll open up our hands and let those old feelings drift right up to Jesus so He can take care of them for us." EJ nodded, and opened his hand, palm up. "Okay, you ready? We'll each pray quietly, and when you're done, close your hand, okay?"

Ty watched, his heart aching as the boy bowed his head. Ty closed his eyes, searching for the strength to do what he'd just instructed EJ to do—release his fear and guilt into the Almighty's care. Was it really as simple as he'd told the boy? Slowly, Ty opened his heart and soul, seeking the freedom from guilt only God could provide. When he opened his eyes, EJ's little fist was clenched tightly. Ty realized his own fingers had curled inward. "Okay, EJ. Let's open our hands and let those feelings go."

Together they unfurled their fingers. Ty had come up with the symbolic ritual for the boy's sake, but as he opened his palm and raised it, a sense of lightness washed through him. He glanced down at EJ to find the boy's face free from worry, a small smile on his lips.

He hugged him close. "Feel better now?" EJ nodded firmly. "Good. But you have to promise that you'll still talk to your mom about this. It's important she knows how you feel."

They were walking back toward the cabin when Ginger appeared around the corner.

"How does the new pole work? Did you catch anything?" Her cheery smile faded quickly as she looked at them.

EJ glanced up at Ty. He smiled down at the boy and urged him forward. "Do you want me to get you started?" EJ nodded. "Ginger, Elliot needs to talk to you about some things. I'll be in the boathouse."

EJ walked toward his mother, then stopped and turned around. "You could talk to her, too, Tyster. She's a good listener."

Caught off guard, Ty had to swallow the lump in his throat before responding, "That's a good idea, buddy. Thanks." Unable to meet Ginger's curious gaze, he walked away.

Ginger rested her elbows on the kitchen counter, her chin in her hands. How could she have been so blind? Elliot's confession about his feelings of guilt had ripped her heart to shreds. It had never occurred to her that he would blame himself for her husband's shooting. She ached at the thought of the heavy burden he must have carried for the past few years. If it hadn't been for Ty, she might never have known.

Inhaling a shaky breath, she straightened, clasping her hands tightly in front of her. She and Elliot had talked a long time before she'd sent him to bed. Maybe this was the reason God had brought them to Dover—to clean the slate, remove the rubble from the past few years and level the ground so they could start over, free of the past. She sent up a prayer of thanks and gratitude for landing in Dover, and for putting Ty Durrant in their path.

But how would she ever repay him for all he'd done for them? His friendship, his support, but mostly for taking EJ under his wing. She needed to thank him for helping her son. Pulling her aqua sweater from the hook, she slipped it on and headed for the boathouse.

"It's open."

Ginger stepped into the dim interior, her gaze finding Ty. He sat at the small dining table, forearms resting on the top, his shoulders hunched forward. He looked over at her, one corner of his mouth curving upward. "I thought you might be dropping by. How's EJ? Did he talk to you?"

She nodded, joining him at the table. "He did. I'm still in shock that he blamed himself for John getting injured."

"Did you explain it to him?"

"I think he understands now, but it breaks my heart knowing he was so scared and frightened for so long."

"Did your husband go back inside for a new toy like EJ thought?"

Ginger shook her head. "That's not how it happened at all. He went back in because he'd been given the wrong change." She gathered her thoughts. "Ty, I want to thank you for what you've done for my son. I can't tell you how much it means to me. I wanted to believe Elliot would talk to me about anything, but I guess the circumstances were too much for both of us. Your interest in him gave him the courage and the safety to share his fears. Thank you."

She reached out for his hand, but he captured it in his, triggering that lovely rush of electricity through her nerves. His hand was strong, steady. Dependable. Unnerved by the intensity of her reaction, she pulled free, tugging on her lock of hair. Her gaze fell upon the folder open before him. It looked official. "What are you reading?"

Ty leaned back in his chair, hands resting on his thighs. "The incident report from the shooting. The department shrink has been after me to read it, but I've been putting it off. After talking with EJ this afternoon, I realized I had a few things I needed to confront myself."

"Like this report?" He nodded. "And did it help?"

Ty leaned forward. "The details in this report are very different from what I remember. They're like two unrelated incidents."

"How so?"

"I remember starting back to the car. It was dark. I heard Pete shout. I drew my weapon. Someone appeared around the side of the house with an assault rifle." Ty closed his eyes briefly before going on. "I saw him. I froze. Then I got hit and…that's all. When I woke up in the hospital, they told me Pete hadn't made it. I knew it was my fault. If I hadn't froze, he might still be alive."

Ginger saw his hands shake and reached across the table to touch his arm. "And what about now? After looking at the file?"

"It says there were two shooters. Pete saw the first one and fired, wounding him, but taking a hit." He tapped the folder with one finger. "I saw the second shooter. Pete was already down before I ever saw that kid."

"So it wasn't your fault."

Ty stood and paced off a few steps. "No. Maybe not. But that doesn't change the fact that I froze when I should have acted. What about the next time? What if I get someone else killed because I freeze up?"

Ginger's heart hurt for him. Like EJ, Ty was struggling with undeserved guilt. Ty feared losing his ability the way her son feared losing her love. "Surely, now that you've read the report, you can see it wasn't your fault. Just like EJ wasn't at fault for John's injuries."

Ty ran a hand through his hair. "Yeah, I guess."

He met her gaze, his blue eyes still holding shadows of doubt and sadness. The look was so similar to EJ's a short while ago, her heart warmed. She stood and went to him, touching her palm to the side of his face, the stubble on his cheek drawing her eyes to his angular jaw and to the jagged scar on his neck. "You're a good man, Ty. An honorable man, and a brave one. What you did for my son was brave. I know you'll find your way soon. You're more than a cop, Ty. Much more."

He raised his hand and laid it over hers as it rested against his face. His other hand slipped around her waist and urged her closer. She didn't resist.

"EJ was right. You are a good listener. You're an amazing woman, Virginia Sloan. You take my breath away with your compassion and your courage."

Ginger's knees weakened. Standing close to Ty, eyes locked, she could feel the rise and fall of his chest beneath her hand. When he took her palm from his face and kissed it, her heart raced violently. He said her name softly and leaned his head closer. But she suddenly remembered they were alone, in the confines of a tiny room, and the feelings Ty was stirring in her had no place in her thoughts. She stepped away from him. "I'd better go. It's late and I…"

She turned and hurried out, back to the cabin. Her heart was already in danger, and she worried that taking their relationship beyond friendship would be a huge mistake. She'd made far too many of them in her life. Now, as she stood on the threshold of a second chance, she refused to make a wrong turn.

No matter how much she loved him.

Ty watched Ginger hurry out of the boathouse. He couldn't continue this way—torn between two choices. He either committed to his job or walked away and sought a future with Ginger. But he could do neither until he broke the grip of fear that immobilized him. He forced himself to take a few deep breaths and regain control.

His gaze drifted to the report on the table. He may not be responsible for Pete's death, but what about the next time? He still couldn't pick up his weapon. Anger and frustration swelled in his chest. He swiped the folder off the table and threw it onto the floor. He raked his fingers in his hair. He had to decide soon, because he was nearly out of time.

The Stanton property was overrun with people and vehicles when Ginger arrived Thursday. So many people had turned out to help. People from the local churches, friends and acquaintances of the Stantons, others who were beneficiaries of Handy Works and welcomed a chance to repay the local ministry for their assistance.

And the calls were still coming in. Not only donations of services, but people offering linens, kitchenware and household goods. The local grocer had pledged to stock the pantry. She hadn't seen Ty at all today. With only a few days until Mr. Stanton's release from the hospital, everyone was working extra hours.

Ginger pulled a casserole from the backseat, shutting the door with her hip, then started toward the garage. She smiled when she saw the tables already bulging with delicious dishes to feed the volunteers. She spotted Laura in the distance. She waved and jogged to her side. "What are you doing here? You're getting married in two days."

"That's all under control. Ginger, you've got to help me."

The worry in her friend's eyes concerned her. "What's wrong?"

Laura took a deep breath. "I need you to play at my wedding."

"What? But you said your friend from college was going to play. What happened?"

"Her mother had a stroke, and she can't leave her. Please say you'll fill in. I've been looking for a way to include you." She touched Ginger's arm. "You and EJ are practically family. Please."

Practically family. If only. "All right. I'd be honored. But I'll need to get the music so I can practice."

Laura exhaled a heartfelt sigh. "Thank you. You're a lifesaver. And a good friend. This means you're a member of the wedding party, and you and EJ can come to the rehearsal dinner."

Ginger suddenly realized her acceptance created an additional obstacle. "Laura, I don't really have anything appropriate to wear. I was planning on wearing a simple skirt and blouse, but now..."

"Don't worry. Shelby or I should have something you can borrow."

Ginger raised her eyebrows and took a step closer to Laura. She stood several inches taller than the petite contractor, which meant she was also taller than Shelby. "Really?"

Laura looked her up and down, her expression revealing her understanding. "Oh. I see your point."

Ginger swallowed her pride once again. "I'm so please you asked me, Laura, but I splurged on Elliot's bike. There's just not much left over for extras. Maybe you should find someone else."

Laura shook her head. "No. But I do have an idea. There's a consignment shop in Sawyer's Bend. That's the next town over. We'll go over there and see what they have. I'm sure you can find a dress and shoes for next to nothing. We'll go right after you get off work. I'll pick you up."

Later that day, Ginger and Laura strolled through the consignment store captivated by the vast assortment of nice clothing and jewelry. A quick check of price tags buoyed her hopes. The prices would fit in her tight budget, and she did want to look nice for the wedding. Helping Laura gave her an opportunity to repay the Durrants for their generosity.

With Laura's help, Ginger selected a figure-flattering blue dress, shoes and a necklace and matching earrings from the consignment store. Glancing down at the bags in her hand, Ginger smiled. She'd forgotten what it felt like to wear nice clothes. Her parents had always spoiled her in that regard. She'd had the latest styles and the coolest fashions. That had all ended when she'd married John. Her life had become all about practicality and function.

After placing the packages in the truck of Laura's car, Ginger climbed in and fastened her seat belt. Laura glanced at her with a mischievous grin.

"We have one more stop to make. This one is a gift from me."

When Laura pulled up to a beauty salon, Ginger shot her a puzzled look; but before she could speak, Laura held up a hand. "The woman here is doing the hair for my bridal party. That now includes you."

Ginger shook her head, but Laura quickly touched her arm. "Please, let me do this."

Words of refusal were on the tip of her tongue, but then she thought about how she'd felt in the blue dress. A new hairstyle would complete the picture and boost her self-confidence.

An hour later, Ginger looked at herself in the mirror. The new softer style skimmed her shoulders in layers, and short bangs angled across her forehead. Even her recalcitrant lock of hair had been tamed to look as if it was part of the overall style and not a mistake.

She beamed. One month in Dover had sent her life in a new direction. EJ's, too. She touched her hair. What would Ty think of the transformation? Suddenly, it was very important that he find her attractive.

Chapter Twelve

Ginger's palms were damp and her nerves dancing as she made her way to the piano in the sanctuary of Peace Community Church Saturday afternoon. She sent up a prayer for composure as she slid onto the wooden bench and flexed her fingers. She wanted to do her best for Laura's sake. She took a moment to sort through the music, then checked her watch. With a quick nod from the wedding planner, Ginger placed her fingers on the piano keys.

As she played, she stole quick glances at the guests being seated, paying closer attention when the Durrant family was ushered forward. Shelby, along with the children, was seated on the groom's side, since Adam had no immediate family attending, and Matt was serving as Adam's best man. Laura had asked her cousin, Annelle, to be her maid of honor.

Ty and EJ took seats in the second row on the bride's side. EJ waved, and she gave him a smile in return. He looked adorable in the sport coat he wore. Finally, Mrs. Durrant was escorted to the front row. She looked beautiful in a pale green dress that complemented her blue eyes.

As Ginger began Pachelbel's Canon in D, the guests

rose to honor the bride. She stole a glance at Adam, standing tall in his tux, his nervousness clearly evident in the way he fidgeted with his hands. Laura, escorted by her father, finally arrived in front of the minister. She looked gorgeous in a long lace gown, carrying a bouquet of white tulips.

Mr. Durrant handed his daughter to her groom, then took his seat. Adam's dark good looks were the perfect complement to his bride's honey-blond tresses, which she'd left loose and wavy.

As they repeated their vows, Ginger tried to recall her own marriage ceremony, but little came to mind. It had been an impulsive trip to a justice of the peace; nothing special. When she married again, she wanted something similar to this ceremony. Elegant, yet simple, with only close friends and relatives in attendance. She wanted the vows given by someone ordained into God's work. Official. Special. Memorable.

Her gaze drifted to Ty, instantly envisioning him in a tux, standing at her side. His eyes met hers, sending a rush of heat into her cheeks and causing her hands to tremble. The look in his blue eyes told her his thoughts mirrored her own.

Ty strolled toward the refreshment table, deliberately turning his back on the happy people celebrating his sister's marriage. The joyful tone of the reception was grating on his nerves. While he was happy for his sister, he wasn't in the right frame of mind to appreciate the moment. He took the cola and turned to face the guests again. Laura and her new husband were glued to each other's side, smiling like kids. His gaze slid to his parents, seated at one of the tables, talking with their grandchildren. Across the room, Matt and Shelby held hands like the newlyweds they were.

A sudden sense of isolation choked him. He didn't belong here. They were his family, but in many ways he had nothing in common with them. He scanned the room, searching out one particular face. He found her standing near the entrance talking to Pastor Jim. As if sensing his gaze, she looked up, her green eyes locking with his. She smiled, lifting her hand slightly.

She looked incredibly beautiful in a blue dress that skimmed her curves. She'd done something to her hair. It was all soft and floating around her face, and he longed to touch it.

Music began to play from the DJ's sound system, a slow, romantic ballad. Ty saw his sister take her new husband's hand and lead him to the dance floor. After a few minutes alone on the floor, his parents joined them.

Before he realized what he was doing, he was halfway across the room, his focus on Ginger. He told himself she probably felt a bit awkward, not knowing many of the guests, but he realized as he drew close he was the one who needed to connect with a friendly face. Someone who understood. And right now all he wanted was to hold her in his arms,. A sudden thought brought him up short. Ginger was the only one he wanted in his life. Forever.

She smiled at him, filling his being with inexpressable joy. "You look amazing." Not exactly smooth, but his brain wasn't functioning properly. A pretty blush tinged her soft cheeks.

"Thank you. I've been looking for you."

Encouragement. He took her hand. "Come, dance with me."

On the floor, he took her in his arms, gazing on her lovely face. "You look beautiful."

She met his eyes. "So do you."

He chuckled. "You think I'm beautiful?"

"I think you're the most handsome man in the room."

She drew closer, and he curled his hand around hers, cradling it on his chest, inhaling the heady fragrance of her perfume. She fit so perfectly against him, he wanted to keep her there forever.

Suddenly the room was too crowded. He wanted her all to himself. Taking her hand, he led her off the dance floor and out to the patio, not stopping until he found a secluded corner. He rested his hands at her waist. "What did you do to your hair? It's different."

"Do you like it?"

"Yes, but what happened to that one curl?"

"She fixed it so it wouldn't stick out."

"I liked it sticking out. I like the way it curled around my finger."

"It'll grow back."

"But I'm not sure my heart will. You've stolen it. Completely." He pulled her to him and kissed her, revealing his heart and his love.

Ginger slipped her arms around his neck, melting against him, his strong arms the only thing keeping her upright. Never had she known such a connection, such safety. The promise in his kiss fulfilled her deepest dreams. Breathless, she pulled back, savoring the feelings swirling inside.

She opened her eyes when his fingers gently touched her cheek.

"Ginger, I've fallen in love with you."

His admission filled her with joy, but it also stirred up long-held fears. Her heart soared, her own feelings for him swelling, pushing every other thought aside. "I think I fell in love with you that first night."

"So, what are we going to do about it?"

She pulled away. "Ty, I'm not sure what we feel for each other is enough." The hurt in his eyes pierced her heart. She took another step back. "We're going in two different directions. I'm leaving for Arizona at the end of the week. And you'll be going back to Dallas."

"I don't know that for certain."

"Are you going to leave law enforcement?"

"Maybe. I've already talked to some recruiters about a few jobs."

"Would you truly be happy doing something else?" His silence told her all she needed to know. "You wouldn't. And it's not a life I can contemplate. I can't live with the constant worry—the fear that something might happen to you."

"So are you saying there's no hope for us at all?"

"I can't see a way around the obstacles." She lifted her hand to his face. "Oh, but I wish there was. I do love you, Ty."

The pain in his blue eyes tore her heart to shreds. He took her arm and steered her back inside the reception hall. He led her to the first table and released her. "Let me know when you're ready to go home." He walked off. It was not the way she wanted it. It was the way it was.

Unable to watch him walk away, she sank onto a chair, fighting tears. Somehow she had to make it through the next few days, then she'd be on her way to her mother's. Tomorrow was the welcome-home celebration for the Stantons. Her car would be ready in a few days. Her mother was eager to see them. In a few short days, she and EJ would be on the road to Arizona, and Dover and the people there would fade in their memories.

Sadness tightened her throat. Ty Durrant would never become a faded memory. She'd been a fool to allow herself to fall in love. Now she and EJ would both be hurt. She should have accepted Ty's offer to fly home weeks ago, then none of this would have happened. Now it was too late.

Every nerve in Ginger's body tingled as she waited for the van to come up the Stantons' driveway. Glancing around, she found Ty standing with Shaw near the front of the house. He'd attended the early service, explaining he had to get to the Stantons' to make sure everything was prepared for the homecoming; but she suspected that was simply an excuse to avoid her. Their friendship had taken on an awkward tone. While they couldn't move forward with their relationship, both of them were reluctant to let go completely.

A cheer rose up from the crowd as the van carrying the Stantons pulled up to the front door. Like a scene from a TV show, the whole town of Dover had turned out to welcome them home. The weather was overcast and cool, but nothing could dampen the volunteers' excitement. The van door opened, and the lift gate lowered Mr. Stanton to the ground. He would be in the wheelchair many weeks yet, so a special ramp had been installed at the front of the home for easy access.

Ty appeared at her side, taking her hand in his and sending a warm flush along her nerves. The look in his blue eyes reflected her own mixed emotions—a mixture of affection and sadness. She was glad he was with her to see the culmination of the project. They'd both become emotionally invested in completing the home on time. Together they listened as Mrs. Stanton thanked the crowd, her words moving many to tears, then Shaw and Pastor Jim escorted the family inside their new home.

As the crowd began to disperse, Ty gently steered her toward the SUV. Ginger turned a puzzled gaze in his direction.

He read her thoughts. "I'll take you home."

"I'd like that."

Matt and Shelby had taken EJ and Kenny to a movie, and Ginger had been looking forward to some alone time on the deck, rocking and watching the water. But now she welcomed time with Ty.

They drove home in silence. At the cabin, they strolled across the deck, hand in hand. Ty stopped at the door, bending to give her a quick kiss. A smile softened his blue eyes and chiseled features.

Inside, she headed toward the kitchen, floating on the joy of being close to him again, even if it was for a short while. "How does a cup of coffee sound? I can have it ready in a jiffy."

"Great. I'll make a fire or we can sit on the deck if you'd..."

She turned to look at him, her heart stopping midbeat when she saw him staring at her notebook, the one where she kept track of the money she owed him. He stiffened, the muscle in his jaw flexing rapidly.

Slowly, he turned, piercing her with his angry blue gaze. "What is this?"

Hurrying around the island, she reached for the notebook, but Ty held it out of her grasp.

"Are you keeping track of the money you think you owe me?"

Heat scorched her cheeks. She intended her list to be a thank-you, but the tone in his voice clearly showed he felt differently. "I wanted to pay you back."

"I never asked you to."

"I know, but you didn't ask us here, either. We were forced on you. You came home looking for peace and quiet, and you found a homeless woman and her child living in your cabin. It only seemed fair to compensate you for your inconvenience."

Ty's blue eyes darkened. He held the notebook up with a little shake. "This is more than compensation, Ginger. You've listed every minor expense." He glanced down at the page. "Daily rental fee for cabin. Food. Percentage of utilities. Fee for assembling the bike. Why?"

Ginger wrapped her arms across her middle protectively. She hadn't expected Ty to be so upset. Memories of John's angry outbursts threatened to overwhelm her. "I didn't want to take advantage of you."

Ty closed the journal and dropped it onto the counter with a loud slap. "You're not taking advantage of me."

"Yes, we have. We've barged into your life, lived in your home rent-free, driven your car, never paid for food or gas. You fix things. You take us places. You share your family with us. Yes, I think we've taken advantage of your kindness far too much. All I wanted to do was repay what we've taken from you."

"Taken?" Ty ran a hand through his hair. "You've taken *nothing* from me, Ginger. You and EJ have given me more than I ever expected to find when I came home to Dover. I thought I wanted peace and quiet, but what I really needed was to focus on something other than my problems. I like having you and EJ here. I don't want your money. Don't you understand that I do things for you because I love you?"

She tried to make him understand. "This isn't about money. It's about being in debt. I have to think ahead, be prepared in case something should happen." Anxiety tightened her throat when she saw the fire still burning in his eyes.

Ty set his jaw, taking her shoulders in his hands. "Ginger, you have to let go of this fear that rules your life. You're afraid of debt, you're afraid of some disaster waiting around every corner, you're afraid to love me because something might happen. You've built this wall around your heart and your life, trying to keep you and Elliot safe. I get that, but that wall is also keeping me out."

His words stung like needles. She thought he would understand. "Oh, so now you're an expert on fear? What about *your* fear, Ty? Have you made your decision?"

"That's not the same thing."

"Really? My fear is holding me back. Your fear of failure is keeping your—how did you put it?—your wheels spinning in the mud." Ginger balled her fists at her sides. "I think you'd better leave."

"Ginger..."

She turned her back and walked to the sink. Tears stung the backs of her eyes. Her stomach was churning. She heard his steps as he walked to the door, and the swish of his jacket as he lifted it from the hook.

"I guess you were right. Love isn't enough.There are too many obstacles between us."

The door opened, letting a cool rush of winter air into the room, freezing her heart. The door closed with a snap, and her heart broke in two.

Ginger closed the music books, stacking them neatly on top of the spinet piano. She left the anthem and hymns for Sunday's service on the music stand for the pianist. Choir practice had gone well. Nearly every member had shown up, which meant Sunday's anthem would be full and rich.

She sent up a grateful prayer. Playing for the choir had provided her only moments of joy since Ty had found her journal. He'd avoided her for the past two days. He still picked EJ up from school but disappeared the moment she arrived home, leaving her with a lingering sadness in her soul. Thankfully, EJ appeared unaware of the tension between herself and Ty. April had told her Ty was managing the Handy Works ministry while Laura was away on her honeymoon.

Edith Johnson approached the piano, a friendly smile on her face. "We are so glad you could fill in for Sarah, but I hate that you're leaving us before long."

"Me, too. I've grown very fond of Dover."

"It's a charming place to live, and a wonderful, safe place to raise a family."

Safe. Ginger had to agree. She felt completely safe here in this small town. Something she once doubted she'd ever feel again. Dover had given her a sense of security, along with a connection to family and faith.

"Ginger." Marilyn Smith approached the piano, her husband at her side. "Could we go over our duet once more? I'm just not sure about our harmony from measure twenty-eight on."

Ginger smiled at the couple. Sam and Marilyn Smith were singing during the offertory this week, and both were a little nervous. "Of course. Though I think you have it down perfectly."

Marilyn opened her music. "Well, one more run-through can't hurt."

Her husband chuckled. "Amen to that."

Edith grasped her cane as she turned to face the singers. "Well, I certainly wouldn't mind hearing it again. Mind if I hang around?"

The rest of the choir members slowly drifted out, their conversations fading as they moved into the hallway and out the back door. Ginger selected the music and sat down on the bench.

She ran through the song twice, until the Smiths felt confident with their parts. As she straightened up the music once again, she was vaguely aware of how quiet the room was with only the four of them. Edith was still in front of the piano, looking over Sunday's music. Sam and Marilyn were over near the coat and choir robe rack gathering their things. She was so glad she'd agreed to take this position. She enjoyed every moment, and the people she'd met were an added blessing.

"Don't anybody move, or I swear I'll kill you all."

Ginger froze. Someone screamed. Sam uttered a curse.

"Quiet!"

Her gaze landed on a tall man standing just inside the choir room. His face was contorted with anger, his eyes glassy and dark. He held a gun in his hand. Her mind balked at what was happening. A quick glance at the others told her they were equally shocked and terror-stricken.

Blood chilled in her veins.

"What do you want? There's no money in here."

Sam's question spiked her fear higher. She didn't want to make the man any angrier.

"I want Reed. Where is he?" The gunman scanned the room with his bloodshot eyes. "Why isn't he here? He's supposed to be here."

Ginger swallowed the knot in her throat. She didn't know who he was talking about.

Sam spoke up again. "He didn't come tonight."

A string of loud curses blasted the air. "No! No. He should be here!" The man fumed, pointing his gun at Sam. "Someone is going to pay for this."

A dark storm of fear raged through Ginger's mind. Her safe haven here in Dover was gone—shattered in an instant. Would she ever be free of the danger and the violence?

Chapter Thirteen

Ty fought to maintain his calm as he maneuvered his vehicle toward the church. A glacier of fear had stopped his heart. An armed gunman was holding hostages in the choir room of Peace Community. And Ginger was one of them. He'd dropped Elliot off at his parents' house, explaining only that Ginger needed his help with something at church.

Pulling to a stop near the police perimeter, he climbed out and headed toward Brady. "What do you know?"

"Not much. He won't respond. He's made no demands and hasn't asked to speak to anyone. We have no idea what he wants."

Ty raked a hand through his hair. "Do we know who it is? Someone local? A drifter?"

"Chief." An officer approached from the far side. Ty recognized him as Vince Butler. They'd spoken a few times in the gym. "We've identified the man. It's Andy Stringer."

Ty knew the name. "Stringer. I played basketball in high school with a Stringer."

Vince nodded. "That's him."

"Taking hostages doesn't sound like the guy I knew. Any idea what's going on with him?"

Brady shook his head. "Nope. But I intend to find out."

Ty paced as Brady issued orders to check out Stringer. His thoughts were consumed with Ginger. Was she all right? Had she been harmed? She must be terrified. He wished there was some way to reassure her. When Brady returned, Ty grabbed his arm. "Have you called in your negotiator? You need to open a dialogue with this guy. Make a connection and find out what he wants before someone gets hurt."

"We don't have a negotiator. In case you've forgotten, we're a small police force. We don't deal with this much here. I've put in a call for a man from Jackson to come down."

"No. That will take too long. We need to get on top of this now." Ty rubbed a hand over his jaw. "I can do it. I've worked a couple of hostage situations. Besides, I know this guy. He'll talk to me."

Brady shook his head. "You knew him years ago. Besides, you're not authorized."

"There's no law that says a negotiator has to be a professional. I have more experience than anyone else here." Ty could see his friend weighing his options. "Brady, Ginger is in there."

"Fine, but we've already tried talking to him. He won't answer." Brady handed Ty the bullhorn.

"Andy Stringer. It's Ty Durrant. I want to talk to you."

A shadow moved across the choir room window. "Tyler. Is that you?"

"Yeah. What's going on, Beano?"

"I thought you were a cop in California."

"Texas, but I'm not a cop now. Just a friend who

doesn't want to see anyone hurt. Why don't you come out so we can talk?"

Silence. "You come in. Alone. Then we'll talk."

Brady grabbed Ty's arm. "Don't even think about it. That's not protocol."

"I'm not interested in procedure. I'm interested in getting those people out safely. I'll do what I have to."

Brady grumbled under his breath, "I can't let you go in there. My head will be on the chopping block."

"I know what I'm doing." Ty raised the bullhorn again. "Andy, I don't like yelling through this thing. I know one of the people with you. I'm going to call her cell. You answer, and we'll work something out. Okay?" Ty held his breath, praying his old friend would cooperate.

"Yeah. Okay."

Ty pulled out his cell and dialed Ginger's number, his heart racing in his chest as he waited to hear her voice.

"Hello?"

Ty braced himself against the fear in her voice. He couldn't think about that now. "Ginger, give the phone…" A screech. Ty's stomach lurched.

"Ty?"

He recognized Andy's voice. "Hey, buddy. What's going on with you? Why don't you come out and we'll catch up?"

"No! You come in. I'm tired of talking on the phone, being put on hold and ignored."

"Okay, sure. I'm coming right now." Ty ended the call and started to slip the phone into his pocket. Brady held out another phone.

"Take this one. It's a direct line to me."

Ty nodded and headed toward the building. At the back door his hand slid automatically to his hip, but there was no weapon there. A cold sweat broke out on his skin. His hands shook. The sense of vulnerability hit him. What if he failed again? What if he froze when Ginger needed him? He sent up a prayer for strength and courage. He couldn't give in to the fear and doubt. Ginger and the others were depending on him.

Stringer was waiting, gun drawn, as Ty stepped inside. One glance told him his old friend was drunk and desperate. Not a good combination. Ty kept his hands in plain view. His posture easy and open.

Andy raked him with a hard gaze. "You wired?"

"No."

"A gun?"

Ty offered a friendly smile. "Nope. I'm not a cop in Dover. I have a phone they want me to give you in case you want to ask for something." Slowly, Ty pulled the phone from his pocket and held it up. Stringer snatched it from him and motioned him into the choir room.

Ty entered the room, quickly making eye contact with each of the hostages. His gaze lingered an extra moment on Ginger. She looked pale and tense, but otherwise okay. The others were equally frightened but calm. Training kicked in.

He studied Andy a moment, assessing his level of anger. High. He'd have to give him time to calm down and rethink his actions. "Want to tell me what's troubling you, Beano?"

Stringer's eyes widened. "No one has called me that in a long time."

Ty chuckled softly. "All-county forward for the Dover Gators. Six feet four and skinny as a string bean."

The gun in his hand waivered slightly. "Yeah, that's how I got the name Beano."

"Good times."

Stringer tensed. "Not anymore. Good times are gone. They took my life and I want it back." He paced across the room.

"Tell me, what happened? Maybe we can find a solution, and let these folks go home."

"No! They're staying. Nobody leaves. Not until I get everything fixed. Not until they give me back what they took."

"Who are *they?*"

Stringer rubbed his head, the gun in his hand waving back and forth. "The people at work. They laid me off after twelve years. That's not right." He pointed the gun at Ty. "I wanted to talk to the banker. He's supposed to be here."

"Why the banker?"

"He stole my house. I tried talking to them, but they wouldn't listen. They wouldn't give me a chance to come up with the money."

"That's rough, buddy. I know you're angry, but maybe you and I can sort this all out."

"Too late. I lost my family, too. Jennifer took the kids and moved to Biloxi with her mother. Now I've got nothing!"

Ty nodded with understanding. "So, what can we do to help?"

Stringer took a step toward him. "I want my house back."

The way his old friend carelessly handled the weapon told Ty he had no experience with firearms. A drunk, angry man with a loaded weapon was the worst-case scenario. "Okay, maybe we can get in touch with this guy, and see what we can work out. But first, we have to end this situation. Why don't we let these people go home? They're not part of this."

For a moment, Ty thought he might agree, but the man's anger and frustration kicked in again.

"No! Not until I get my job and my house back."

Edith quietly sobbed. Ty saw Ginger reach over and take her hand. Stringer saw it, too, and pointed the gun in their direction. Ty's heart stopped. It took all his determination to remain calm. He fell back on his training. It was clear the older woman was reaching her limit.

"Hey, Beano, what say you let Mrs. Johnson go?"

"No."

"You know her, pal. Miss Edith makes those amazing chocolate chip cookies that everyone in Dover can't get enough of."

"Yeah, I know them."

"Don't you want to have a few when you leave here? Let her go, so she can make more cookies."

Ty held his breath, taking care to keep his body language open and friendly, his features in a calm, understanding expression.

"Yeah, okay. But no one else. Got it? Not until someone fixes the mess they've made of my life!"

"Good. Ginger, why don't you help Miss Edith to the door, and let the officers outside take you home." Ty prayed Stringer was too drunk and too stressed to see the ploy until it was too late. No such luck.

"Stop. You're trying to trick me into letting them both go. You take the old lady to the door, then come back."

Ty helped Mrs. Johnson to the back door and handed her off to the officer, giving him a small nod to signal everything was okay. When he returned to the choir room, Ginger caught his gaze. Her fear tore at his heart. He longed to go and reassure her he'd protect her, but he had a job to do first.

* * *

Ginger exhaled a tense breath as Ty reentered the choir room. Her mind ricocheted between relief that he was here and fear that his actions could cost him his life. Why did he always have to rush into danger? Why did he feel so compelled to help others?

"Get over here." The man aimed the gun at Ty.

She struggled to breathe around the fear lodged in her throat. She sent up a prayer for his safety, for the hostages' safety, and a few requests she couldn't even form into words.

Gesturing with the gun, Stringer motioned Ty to stand in front of him. Ginger's heart stopped.

"The rest of you go sit in the chairs where I can keep an eye on you."

Ginger and the Smiths made their way to the first row of chairs and sat down. Stringer ordered Ty to sit down, too. Ty picked up a chair from the bottom riser, positioning it between his old friend and the hostages.

A scream fought its way up her throat. Ty was placing himself directly between the gunman and the hostages. A gesture declaring he was willing to die to protect them.

"So, tell me what we can do to end this standoff. I can't help you if you don't know what you want."

Ginger's nerves quivered. How could Ty remain calm in this situation? He behaved as if he didn't have a care in the world.

"I want that man Reed. Davis Reed at First Dover Trust."

"Okay, let's call him up and see what he has to say."

"He won't answer."

"He will if the chief of police calls him. You can use that phone I gave you. Brady Reynolds will get him here."

Stringer considered the idea a moment, then tossed the phone to Ty. "You call."

"Sure." Ty pressed a button and waited.

Ginger finally understood what Ty was doing. Keeping calm, displaying a friendly attitude, that was giving the man time to defuse his anger. Seeing Ty in action gave her a deeper insight into the man she'd come to love. He truly was called to this profession. He had the temperament, the passion and the ability. For the first time she understood why he struggled to leave a job he loved.

Stringer paced like a caged animal while they waited, and Ty could see he was wavering. Ty fought the pull to make eye contact with Ginger. He had to keep his attention on him. He was becoming agitated again as they waited for Brady to call back. "Andy, you don't want to do this. If we stop right now, it can all be worked out. I'll find someone to help you. But you have to give yourself up and let these people go."

He shook his head. "People always promise they'll help, but they don't. God promises things, and He turns away when you really need Him. He lets bad stuff happen when He could stop it with just a thought. I've been a good Christian all my life, and He took it all away."

The fury behind the guy's eyes alarmed him. He didn't want this situation to escalate. "I'm promising you now. I'll look into it. I'll stay on top of it. You know how stubborn I can be when I put my mind to something."

The phone rang, and Stringer grabbed it from Ty's hand. He mumbled a few curt responses, then moved to the window, keeping his gun on Ty. After a quick glance outside, he shoved the phone into his pocket, taking a position near the door again.

"What did they say?"

"He's here. Outside. He says he'll try and work something out about the house."

"That's great. Maybe this was all a misunderstanding, huh?" His friend looked at him, eyes filled with sorrow.

"I guess."

Ty knew the moment Stringer decided to give up. "Give me the gun, Beano. We'll call the chief and tell him we're coming out, okay?"

Stringer stared at him a long moment, and Ty feared his anger might ratchet up once more. Finally, he sighed and held out the weapon, the dejected slope of his shoulders signaling his surrender. Ty stepped forward, took the gun and ejected the clip. The familiar action brought with it his old sense of confidence and a realization that his decision had been made. Stringer sank down onto the chair, head bowed.

Ty ached to go to Ginger, but he couldn't until Stringer was in custody. Ty called the chief, then took Stringer's arm and urged him to his feet.

"What happens now? Am I going to jail?"

Ty glanced up as Dover police officers entered the room. "For now. But it'll all get sorted out. I'll be there with you."

Free at last, Ty turned to see the Smiths being led away. Ginger stood, talking to a female officer. He moved toward her, dismissing the other officer. She fell into his arms immediately. He held her tightly against his chest, her head resting under his chin. She trembled against him, and he pulled her closer. "Are you all right?" She nodded. "You were very brave. I'm proud of you. You kept everyone calm."

She held him more tightly. "I was so scared."

"He didn't want to hurt anyone. He was angry and frustrated and didn't know where to turn."

She shook her head. "Not for me. For you."

His heart swelled in his chest. Her concern for him touched him deeply. "I'm so sorry you had to go through that." He felt her relax against him.

"Can we go home now? I need to see Elliot."

Ty wrapped an arm around her shoulder. "He's at Mom and Dad's. I told them to keep this from him until you could explain it in person."

"Thank you." She raised her eyes and looked into his.

His heart swelled, then thudded in his chest. He kissed her lightly on the lips, then gently turned her toward the door. "You'll need to give a statement to the police, but I'll come with you. Or I can make arrangements for you to talk to them tomorrow if you'd like."

"No. I want it over with, so I can go home."

Home. Did she mean the cabin or her mother's?

Ginger's heart rate had finally returned to normal but left her feeling drained and shaken. Ty squeezed her hand again. He'd touched her hand several times on the short ride to his parents' home, as if seeking reassurance she was all right. Elliot was waiting on the back porch when they pulled into the driveway and ran to meet her as she got out of the car.

"Mom, they said you were having trouble at the church with some guy. What happened?"

Ginger pulled him close. "A man came into the church. He was very upset and angry. He had a gun."

His eyes grew wide. "A bad guy? Like the one who shot Dad?"

"Yes. But Ty came in and talked to him, and made him give up the gun."

"Ty saved you?"

"Yes. He did. He's was a real hero."

EJ darted to Ty and hugged him. "I love you, Tyster."

Ginger's heart lurched. Tonight had changed everything. But she knew what her future would be, and she knew without a doubt what Ty's would be. They would be going in different directions. How was she going to tell her son that Ty wasn't going to be part of their lives anymore?

Ty stole a glance at Ginger seated beside him in the SUV. She'd been silent and withdrawn during the ride home. Something had changed between them, and he had a sick feeling in his gut that he knew what it was. He just wasn't sure how Ginger knew.

Focusing on the road ahead, he finally faced the truth. From the moment he'd reached out and taken the gun from Beano's hand, his fear had vanished. His mind had cleared. But his realization would cost him the people he loved most.

Ginger slid out of the car the moment it came to a stop at the cabin, urging EJ up the steps, reminding him that tomorrow was still a school day. Ty followed at a distance, giving them space to talk. In the cabin, he heard Ginger and EJ in the bedroom. Taking the tea pitcher from the fridge, he poured a glass and sat down at the counter to wait for Ginger.

Ty glanced up as she came into the kitchen, her expression showing her surprise that he was there. She avoided his gaze and moved to the sink. Wetting down a rag, she began wiping the counter. "Ginger, we need to talk."

She shook her head, keeping her back to him. "No. Not tonight. I'm too upset."

"Talking about it helps. I'm here for you. You know that." He saw her shoulders tense.

"Please. I need time alone to sort through all this."

Clearly, she wasn't going to let him help. Exhaling a slow sigh, he stood. "All right. We'll talk tomorrow." He turned and walked toward the door but stopped when she called his name.

"Thank you for keeping us all safe tonight."

He turned to look at her, his gaze caressing her lovely face. She looked vulnerable, lost and confused. He longed to hold her close and chase away her fears. "I'd keep you safe forever if I could." Tears suddenly appeared in her eyes. He took a step toward her, but she backed up, shaking her head.

Ty rubbed his neck, turned and left the cabin. Maybe she was right. Tomorrow everything would look different.

Ginger stirred the spaghetti sauce slowly to keep it from sticking to the bottom of the pan. Ty stood beside her, slicing vegetables for the salad. The simple, familiar routine gave her a measure of security and comfort. Still, she wished Ty wasn't here. She knew he was itching to talk about last night, but she wasn't. She'd avoided him today by leaving for work early and coming home late, hoping to forestall this discussion altogether. Tomorrow she and Elliot were leaving for Arizona. She wasn't looking forward to telling Ty. Or EJ, for that matter. She'd tell him in the morning.

The meal was quiet and awkward. EJ did most of the talking, which suited her fine. But once her son was tucked in bed, she knew time had run out. Ty was waiting for her on the sofa, feet propped up on the ottoman, a cozy fire in the fireplace. This was going to be harder than she'd imagined.

He looked at her, and from the stern set of his jaw and the darkened shade of his blue eyes, she knew it was time to confront the elephant in the room. She took her time joining him, sitting as far from him as possible on the sofa. She sensed him searching for a place to start and decided to take the initiative.

"I understand it now."

"What?"

"Who you are. Last night I saw firsthand what you're born to do. You're supposed to help and protect others. What happened last night cleared everything up for you, didn't it?"

Ty gazed into her eyes, a deep puzzled frown creasing his proud forehead. "Yes. It did." He shook his head. "I can't give it up, Ginger."

She swallowed her last morsel of hope. "I know, and I would never ask you to. It would be cruel and unfair."

Ty leaned toward her. "And what does that mean for you and me? I love you."

"And I love you, too, but Ty, I need security. A safe place to live my life and for EJ to grow up. I thought it might be here with you, in Dover, but even here there's no safety." Tears filled her eyes. She wiped them away. "I need to go home, to my mother's. I know it sounds childish and irrational, but I need her right now. We've been separated for so long. EJ needs a family."

"*I* want to be his family."

Ginger sucked in a sharp breath. She didn't need to hear this now. It was too painful. "No, it won't work. We're going in two different directions. You're heading back into danger, and I can't live knowing you might not come home one day. I can't risk putting EJ through losing another father."

"I wish..."

"No. Don't." She stood and moved away. "I won't let you regret this decision. God has given you a purpose, and you have to fulfill it, Ty. I want you to go back to being a cop. It'll make me happy knowing you're doing what you love."

"And what about you?"

"I'm going to my mom's, and we're going to catch up on all the lost years, and she's going to get to know her grandson. I'll find a job and try to put the past behind me."

"Ginger, maybe we can..."

"Ty, please understand. I have to be safe. I have to find a place where I can stop worrying about the next disaster, the next threat. I can't live through the uncertainty again." She pressed her hands against her abdomen. "My stomach is in knots just thinking about it."

Ty stood and came to her side. "So you're just going to walk away. Forget this month ever happened? Forget me?"

"No. Not you. Not Dover." Leaving him, leaving Dover, was going to be one of the hardest things she'd ever done. "Dallas isn't that far from Phoenix. You could come visit. Once we're settled."

"Sure." Ty turned away, running a hand through his hair. "Maybe EJ can come to Dallas. I could take him to a ball game."

"He'd like that."

"Would you come with him?"

"I don't think that would be a good idea." Ty reached

out for her, but she held up her hands and stepped back. "You'd better go. Please." She looked down at her hands. They were shaking. "We'll be leaving tomorrow."

"So soon? But your job isn't finished."

"I talked to Pastor Jim today. He understands." She braved a look in his blue eyes. "Please, Ty. I need to go home." He hesitated for a moment, then nodded, sending a wave of regret through her heart. A small part of her wanted him to stop her from leaving.

"I understand." He walked to the door and stopped. He looked over his shoulder at her. "Goodbye, Ginger."

The door closed behind him as her tears fell.

Chapter Fourteen

He couldn't watch them drive away. He couldn't bear the thought of them not being at the cabin, so he'd covered his heartbreak the only way he knew how—by helping. First thing this morning he'd gone to the storage shed and started transferring all her belongings to the car. Every item he stowed was one less link to Ginger and EJ. And yet, another part of him was strangely at peace. He knew now he truly belonged in law enforcement. But it required a painful sacrifice—losing the two people he loved most in the world.

Ginger wanted what was best for him. She wanted him to be happy. And he wanted that for her, too. She needed her family, she needed to find safety, and what better place than with the mother she'd lost so long ago? So, if they both wanted what was best for each other, why did it hurt so much? His heart was wrenched in two, confident of his future, but devastated by the cost.

He repacked the car twice before accepting EJ's bike wasn't going to Arizona. He set it aside just as the boy rounded the corner. The realization and disappointment in the boy's eyes cut Ty deep. "Sorry, buddy. I'll ship it to you. Promise."

"You could bring it yourself."

Ginger appeared behind him, setting her suitcases on the ground, then placing her hands on her son's shoulders. "Elliot. Ty's going back to work, remember?" He nodded. "Time to say goodbye. We need to be going."

EJ ran to him, wrapping his arms around his waist. Ty lifted him up, hugging him tight against his chest. "I'll miss you, buddy."

"I love you, Tyster."

"I love you, too, EJ." Ty set him down, blinking away the moisture threatening to cloud his vision. Ginger motioned her son into the car, then came toward him. When Elliot was buckled in, she looked up at him, her eyes moist with unshed tears. "Thank you, Ty. For everything. For helping us. For taking care of things, for sharing your family. For saving my life." The tears trickled down her cheek. "I can never…tell you…" She lowered her head, and he pulled her close.

"I know. Me, too." He kissed her forehead, letting his hand trail down her cheek and wrapping her stray curl around his finger. "Take care. Be happy and safe, Ginger. I'll be praying for that."

She nodded and stepped away, climbing into the car and starting the engine. He lifted his hand, then turned and walked around the cabin toward the boathouse, the sound of the departing car lingering in his ears like a bugle playing taps.

Safely inside the boathouse, he pulled off his jacket and threw it across the room. What did he do now? How did he forget them? They'd both made the right decision. If the Lord wanted them together, it would have worked out.

His gaze fell upon his old football. The one he and EJ had used until Ty had bought him a smaller one. How could he ever walk into that cabin and not think about Ginger? Or fish on the dock and not long for his little buddy at his side? Maybe it was time to sell the cabin. Cut all ties with Dover. Matt was happy, Laura newly married. He had little in common with them now.

He dropped into the recliner. The old mechanism groaned and creaked when he leaned back. He looked over at his Bible on the table beside the chair. It was open to Psalms. Maybe it was one of the angry ones, where David cried out his frustration to God. He picked it up, reading the first verse his eyes focused on. *Defend the poor and fatherless: do justice to the afflicted and needy. Deliver the poor and needy: rid them out of the hand of the wicked.*

The words spilled over his soul like a soothing ointment, chasing away any doubts and regrets—a confirmation of his decision. He was exactly where he was supposed to be. Tomorrow he'd go back to Dallas and back to his career.

Traffic on Interstate 10 West was thinning out as they left Baton Rouge behind. A full tank of gas ensured they'd make Lafayette, Louisiana, before they had to stop. The more miles she put between herself and Dover, the better. Distance would ease the pain and regret. A quick glance at her son punctured her confidence in her decision. He remained slumped against the car door, refusing to talk.

She reached out and touched his arm. "EJ?"

"I don't see why we had to leave. I liked it there. I had friends. Why couldn't we stay with Tyster?"

Ginger gripped the steering wheel, her own heart aching. "Ty is going back to Dallas and his job as a police detective. He won't be at the cabin anymore, Elliot."

"EJ. My name is EJ now."

"Sorry. I'll try to remember that. It was nice of Ty to give you a special name."

"Tyster's a hero. He protected you from that bad man."

"I know that, but he can't protect us from everything. And I want you to be safe."

"But I am safe. Jesus watches over us all the time. And Tyster will keep you safe, too, because he likes you."

"What makes you say that?"

"He said you're special, and very brave, and I'm lucky to have a great mom like you."

"He said that?"

"Yeah. And then he said he liked to look at you because it made him happy."

Ginger tried not to dwell on what EJ had told her. Looking at Ty made her happy, too. His dazzling smile, the wavy hair, the broad shoulders, so capable and strong. She shut down the images flooding her mind. It didn't matter now.

Elliot focused on his game player for the next hour. Lake Charles, Louisiana, was a short distance ahead. They were over three hours from Dover. So why wasn't the distance making her feel better?

A blue rest area sign flashed by, filling her with a sudden need to talk to her mother. She pulled into the right lane, then eased onto the exit ramp.

"Why are we stopping, Mom?"

"Time to stretch a bit, and I want to call your grandmother and let her know our progress."

"Can I run around under those trees?"

"Sure." Ginger followed him across the grassy area, taking a seat at one of the covered picnic tables. Pulling out her cell, she selected her mother's number. "Hey, Mom."

"Oh, Ginny. Honey, I'm so glad you called. I was going to call you as soon as things calmed down around here."

"What happened?"

Her mother sighed. "Oh, it's awful. Our complex was robbed last night. Three different units were broken into."

Ginger's throat seized up. "Are you okay?"

"Yes, yes. They didn't rob me. But my friend Mary had her jewelry taken, and her TV and other things. It was awful. I'm a nervous wreck."

Tears sprung into her eyes, her chest tightened, making it hard to breathe. "Oh, Mom."

"Honey, don't worry. It's all fine now. The police were here, and they already have a lead on the thief. It's a grandson of one of the neighbors. So sad."

Ginger's hand began to shake. A tidal wave of fear began to swell up from deep inside. "Mom, I'm glad you're all right. I just wanted to let you know that we're in Louisiana. I'll call you later, okay?"

"Honey, are you all right? You sound funny."

"I'm fine. I'll call you soon."

"Don't let this event upset you. Remember to place your trust in the Lord. He loves you even more than I do. Bad things happen all the time, but the good Lord is always by your side, and He'll help you through it all."

Sobs escaped Ginger's throat the second she ended the

call. She buried her face in her hands, fear and hopelessness swamping her mind. There was no peace, no safety anywhere. Even in the idyllic town of Spring Valley, danger and violence had reared its head. Why couldn't she find a safe place to live? Why was God doing all these things to her? She was a good Christian. She'd tried to live a good life, she'd tried to… Her mind froze on an image. The gunman—his face contorted in anger as he blamed God for his situation. She'd found his words ludicrous at the time. God hadn't put the gun in his hand. But what about her situation? God hadn't sent the man into the restaurant just so John could be shot.

So what did that leave? If God wasn't to blame, who was? She thought back over her life and the choices she'd made. Her own youthful resentment and rebellion had turned her away from her family and her faith, not God. So, where did she turn now? Where was her safe place?

Tears spilled down her cheeks, and she dug in her purse for a tissue, coming up with a rumpled one and the small card Pastor Jim had given her on her last day. The picture on the front featured a tall brick tower bathed in a ray of light from above. Phrases of comfort her mother had taught her bloomed in her mind. *Strong tower. Come to me. Peace I give you.*

Like fog lifting on a winter day, she saw her path. There was no city safe enough, no job free from danger, no person she could depend on completely. Only the Lord never changed. He alone had the power to overcome fear. She'd forgotten that and lost her way in the fear created by one violent act.

Ginger let her gaze travel to Elliot playing in the grassy park. She wanted him to be safe always, but now she saw that it wasn't up to her. Mom had told her to trust the Lord. Maybe it was time she took the last step and released all of herself into His care. Like the prodigal son, she'd started toward her Father, and now He was running to meet her, in a rest stop in Louisiana.

Bowing her head, she prayed, giving all her fears, doubts and pain over to the only one strong enough to carry them. When she opened her eyes again, she saw her son, her gaze landing on the ball cap he always wore. The hat Ty had given him.

Wiping her eyes, she remembered her prayer the first night in the cabin. She'd longed for a safe place to start over. The Lord had brought her to Dover and given her Ty. A man who loved her and loved her son as his own. He was a man who would protect them with every fiber of his being. It was all she could ask from a man. God had led her to Dover and restored her peace, shown her a different kind of security, but she'd been too bound by fear to see it.

"Mom, you okay? You crying?"

She reached out and took his hand. "I'm very okay."

"Is it time to go?"

She stood, draping her purse over her shoulder as she turned toward the car. Where should she go? Home to mom or home to Dover? Was it too late? What if Ty had changed his mind? EJ tugged on her arm.

"Mom? Are we going or not?"

She swallowed a lump of anxiety. Which direction did she go?

Ty's SUV was parked near the cabin. Ginger exhaled a sigh of relief. He was here, but how would he feel about them being back? EJ was out of the car before she shut off the engine. He raced up the cabin stairs shouting for

Ty. She got out of the car more slowly, her heart pounding. She had so much to say. But she couldn't let fear keep her from telling him. Fear had stolen too much of her life already.

EJ bounded down the stairs again, racing around to the front of the cabin. She heard him shout for Ty once more. She walked around to the front, her gaze landing on Ty as EJ threw himself into his arms. As she drew nearer, she could see the worry and concern on Ty's face. She smiled, searching his eyes for the welcome she'd hoped for.

He hurried forward, his gaze raking her from head to toe. "Are you all right? What happened? EJ said you're back, but he didn't say why."

She reached out and touched the center of his chest, taking comfort from the solid strength of him. "We realized we needed to come home."

Confusion darkened his blue eyes. "Ginger?"

"Something happened at my mother's, and it made me realize you were right. Fear has dominated my life and kept me from reaching out for what I want most."

"What happened?"

She waved him off. "It doesn't matter. What matters is that I know what I want now." She looked into his eyes. "I want you." Ty sucked in a sharp breath, and for a second she feared she was too late, that he'd changed his mind.

"I thought I'd lost you forever." He pulled her into his arms, his hand cradling the back of her head. "I didn't know how I was going to live without you and EJ."

She allowed herself to bask in his embrace a moment before pulling back. She wanted him to understand. "Ty, I love you, and I'm all right with your job. It's part of who you are. God chose you to do this work, and I'm going to trust Him to protect you."

"Are you sure? I mean—"

She stood on tiptoe and kissed him. "I'm very sure." He crushed her to him, kissing her with a passion that promised a future together.

"I love you."

"I love you, too."

A giggle interrupted them. "You guys were kissing. Yuck. Can I ride my bike?"

Ginger smiled and slipped her arm around Ty's waist. "Sure, but wear your helmet."

Ty looked down at her with a searching gaze after EJ disappeared around the cabin. "Are you sure you want to be a cop's wife? It's not easy."

"I want to be *your* wife. The rest we'll work out."

He pulled her close again. "Well, I think I have a solution that will make things easier for both of us. I just got off the phone with Brady. He's offered me a job here in Dover as the head of the patrol division. I'm seriously considering it."

"Are you sure?"

He reached out and touched the cowlick strand of hair near her cheek. "I realized that serving the people of Dover, the people I care about, gives me more satisfaction than chasing down violent criminals. I want what Matt and Laura have. A family and a home. With you and EJ. Marry me. Let's start our life together here in Dover."

"Yes. When? Tomorrow?"

Ty laughed. "Tomorrow? I thought you'd at least want time to plan a big wedding."

She shook her head. "I want a simple wedding with Pastor Jim and your family. How about Valentine's Day?"

"That's only two weeks away."

"I know, but maybe your family will help me pull it together."

"You know they will." He hugged her close, kissing the top of her head. "Then all that's left is to buy a plane ticket."

"Why?"

"So your mother can be here to help you plan. She'll be disappointed you aren't going to Spring Valley after all."

She reached up and touched his cheek. "You really do think of everything. Thank you. I called her and told her I was coming back to Dover. I think she knew why."

"All that's left is a ring and a place to live."

"We can live in the cabin."

"Laura's selling her house. I thought it might make a nice family home."

"It would be the perfect place." Ginger had never believed she could be so happy or feel so safe. She'd found a home—in Ty's arms.

* * * * *

Dear Reader,

Sometimes when you write a book, you end up reminding yourself of the same truths you've given your characters. Fear is one of the greatest obstacles to our faith. It raises doubts, undermines our belief in our abilities and can keep us from moving forward. I was reminded many times as I told Ty and Ginger's story how quickly I forget the Lord's faithfulness and let fear fill my heart and mind.

Ty and Ginger both faced a life-changing moment as a result of sudden violence. The shooting of her husband left Ginger with an overpowering desire for safety and security. Being shot in the line of duty undermined Ty's confidence in his ability to be a police officer.

Both are struggling to put their lives back together. But Ty, despite his fear, keeps praying and waiting for God to direct him. Ginger blames God for her situation and struggles alone, trying to pay off debt and reach her mother's home in Arizona, where she thinks she'll find a safe place to raise her son. While she's attracted to Ty, falling for a cop, a man who faces the threat of death daily, terrifies her.

As Ty and Ginger develop feelings for one another, their fears prevent them from seeing the gift the Lord has placed in front of them—each other.

I hope Ty and Ginger's story will remind you to put your trust in God, and not let fear keep you from trying something new, or risking your heart, or stepping out of your comfort zone. What He has planned for you is greater than your fears.

Lorraine Beatty

Questions for Discussion

1. Ginger suffered a terrible loss through an act of violence that left her afraid. Sudden changes in our lives often leave us anxious and frightened. If this has happened to you, discuss how you overcame and adjusted to the changes.

2. Fear is probably the greatest obstacle to our peace and happiness. It can also prevent us from making important decisions and keep us stuck in one spot. Have you missed out on some opportunities because of fear of failure or the unknown? If you had to do it over again, what would you do differently?

3. Ginger and Elliot were fortunate to have Ty help them. We don't all have handsome detectives to come to our aid, but we do have people who help when we need it. Tell about a time in your life when others stepped forward to support you when you needed help.

4. Ty has always wanted to be a cop, but being shot destroyed the myth of invincibility he needs to do his job. He's waiting for an answer from above, but it's slow in coming. Why do you think some answers from God take so long?

5. Ginger admires Ty and is attracted to him, but because he's a cop, she could never live with the uncertainty his job would create. Do you think it takes a special kind of person to marry a spouse with a dangerous job?

6. Elliot bonds quickly with Ty. How important is it for children to have good role models?

7. Ginger's desire to reunite with her mother is a driving force. Have you ever been estranged from a loved one? How did you reconcile?

8. Ginger is shocked to learn her son blamed himself for what happened to his father. Why do you think we assume responsibility for certain events even when we shouldn't?

9. The tense situation at church reveals the truth to both Ty and Ginger. Do you think God calls us to certain professions? Why or why not?

10. Ty finally makes his decision about his future, but it might cost him dearly. Have you ever been faced with a choice that came at a high price?

11. What happened that forced Ginger to realize that there is no place free from danger? How did this change her perspective?

COMING NEXT MONTH FROM
Love Inspired®

Available March 18, 2014

THE SHEPHERD'S BRIDE
Brides of Amish Country
by Patricia Davids

Desperate to save her sister, Lizze Barkman turns to formerly Amish Carl King for help. Will she fall for the one person she's forbidden to trust?

A FATHER IN THE MAKING
Hearts of Hartley Creek
by Carolyne Aarsen

Nate Lyster thought he'd never have a family of his own. But beautiful widow Mia Verbeek and her children could change that—if she's willing to make room for the handsome cowboy.

RESCUED BY THE FIREFIGHTER
by Gail Gaymer Martin

Fireman Clint Donatelli had shut the door on relationships. But when he comes to the rescue of pretty Paula Reynolds, will he give love a second chance?

CLAIMING THE DOCTOR'S HEART
Charity House
by Renee Ryan

Olivia Scott is at a crossroads in her life. So when handsome doctor and single dad Connor Mitchel and his twin girls capture her heart, her new path might just be becoming a mother and wife.

PINE COUNTRY COWBOY
by Glynna Kaye

Abby Diaz has returned to Canyon Spings to mend her past. But when she meets charming cowboy Brett Marden, could he be the key to her future?

FINALLY A MOTHER
by Dana Corbit

State trooper Mark Shoffner is happy to reunite Shannon Lyndon with her long-lost son. Can he persuade her to let *him* in her heart?

LOOK FOR THESE AND OTHER LOVE INSPIRED BOOKS WHEREVER BOOKS ARE SOLD, INCLUDING MOST BOOKSTORES, SUPERMARKETS, DISCOUNT STORES AND DRUGSTORES.

LICNM0314

Cowboy, wanderer… Father?

Nate Lyster and Mia Verbeek are in perfect agreement—that letting someone new into your heart is much too risky. Left on her own with four kids, Mia can't let just anyone get close, while wandering cowboy Nate learned young that love now means heartbreak later.

But when a fire turns Mia's life upside down, Nate is the only one who can get through to her traumatized son—and her heart. If Nate and Mia can forget the hurts of their pasts, they might get everything they want. But if they let fear win, a perfect love could pass them by….

A Father in the Making

by

Carolyn Aarsen

Available April 2014 wherever Love Inspired books and ebooks are sold.

Find us on Facebook at www.Facebook.com/LoveInspiredBooks

LI87878